FAMOUS

AFTER

DEATH

FAMOUS

AFTER

DEATH

A NOVEL

BENJAMIN CHEEVER

BLOOMSBURY

In loving memory to Paul Maslin

Published by Bloomsbury Publishing, New York and London.
Distributed to the trade by St. Martin's Press

A CIP catalogue record for this book
is available from the Library of Congress

ISBN 1-58234-087-0

First published in the U.S. by Crown Publishers,
a division of Random House, Inc. in 1999

This paperback edition first published 2000
10 9 8 7 6 5 4 3 2 1

Printed in the United States of America
by R.R. Donnelley & Sons Company, Inc.,
Harrisonburg, Virginia

The man who throws a bomb is an artist,

because he prefers a great moment to anything.

G. K. CHESTERTON

FAMOUS

AFTER

DEATH

From the journals of Noel Hammersmith. The entry is undated but was almost certainly composed in the spring of 1988.

All the prisoners wanted to be on camera. Early this morning, they started banging the bars and stamping their feet, and by the time the crew arrived, the ruckus was deafening. So Candy Ass—that's what we call the warden, Candy Ass—made an agreement with the producer: If the convicts put a lid on it after the interview, the camera would dolly slowly down the line of cells, and everybody could wave and blow kisses.

The Corrections Officers were furious. "You're making scumbags into movie stars! Whose side are you on anyway?" They wanted a ranked shot of the entire prison staff, short ones kneeling in front. The world's fattest, nastiest, and most frequently defeated varsity squad. "Team Cardiac," that's what the prisoners call them.

The producer wouldn't budge. Finally, after a series of angrily whispered conferences, it was agreed that three COs would come on camera to unshackle and then lead me back to my cell. The staff could draw straws to determine which guards got the exposure.

Two armchairs had been set on a raised platform to one side of the common area, so that in a long shot my head would be framed with bars. I believe the network had upholstered the chairs. I saw somebody up here with fabric swatches last week.

Even a homicide has to be prepared for his public. Especially a homicide. The woman who made me up smoked narrow brown cigarettes, smelled of alcohol (was it rubbing alcohol or gin?), and had a wonderfully conspiratorial air. She wore a name tag. "Ms. Mary" it said, and that's how she referred to herself. The guards' toilet, which had been set up as a dressing room, had a sink into which she kept the cold tap splashing noisily throughout our session. "I hope you don't mind, baby," she said. "The sound of water is medicine for my spirit." She touched me with long, cool fingers, on the forehead, behind the ears.

My acne scars were filled in, my hair trimmed. Mascara and eyeliner were lovingly applied. Also, she pinned my uniform up in back, so that it didn't billow, so that my already narrow body seemed even slimmer, imperially slim. Ms. Mary lit one of her cigarettes for me to smoke then she walked around the chair I sat in and gave her labors a final examination. "A star is born." That's what she said.

Barbara Walters was already seated when I was brought onto the set. The guards thought me a relatively harmless individual, and so they weren't frightfully careful about restraints. When I was set down in my chair, and before I was chained, I lurched forward to see if I could make her jump. She jumped all right. So I guess they are real people.

There were a lot of tiresome questions about why I thought quality control was an issue worth killing people for.

"Shoddy workmanship has often been fatal," I said, "in the construction of rocket ships, submarines, and even automobiles. Quality is job one. If I buy a shirt, go home, and yank off the price tag, I'll rip a hole in my new shirt. The monofilament holding the price tag is more durable than the clothing. What is the manufacturer trying to tell me? He is more concerned that the shirt not be stolen than about the shirt itself. This is capitalism gone berserk. In the short run, planned obsolescence is good business. In the long run, it's fatal. In the long run it's man who will become obsolete."

Ms. Walters nodded. "I suspect that much of our viewing audience shares your impatience," she said, with just the touch of schoolmarm in her tone, the real live hornet in the plastic corsage. "But they don't take the law into their own hands. They call the Better Business Bureau, or the local office of Consumer Affairs."

"Have you ever phoned the local office of Consumer Affairs?" I asked. "I called once about Golden Rule Vitamins, Inc. You've seen the Golden Rule advertisements? They're all over the place: 'You have nothing to lose but your shame.' I got a consumer advocate who seemed to have just woken up. I asked if she'd seen the offending advertisements.

"The consumer advocate wanted to know which advertisements.

"The ones where they promise that you'll lose weight while earning thousands of dollars a month in the privacy of your own home.

"The consumer advocate thought she had seen the ads. 'Probably I saw them,' she said.

"I saw them all right," I told her. "I spent more than $600 on diet pills. The advertisement guaranteed that the pounds would melt away.

" 'And they didn't melt away?' she asked.

"Nope," I said. "I actually got fatter.

" 'Oh, dear!' she said.

"Isn't this fraud?" I asked.

"The consumer advocate wouldn't say. 'I'm not a lawyer,' she said. 'I wouldn't want to throw around a word like "fraud." '

"So what should I do?" I asked.

" 'Maybe you should eat less.' That's what she said.

"Get that, Barbara?" I said. "Maybe I should eat less. I need a consumer advocate to tell me to skip dessert? What sort of moron do these people think I am?

"So then I asked if anybody else had ever complained about Golden Rule. That's when she palmed me off on the Better Business Bureau. Out in Westchester a conversation with a real live person at the Better Business Bureau costs $3.80 cents per minute. Plus tax. And you know what he said?"

Barbara didn't know what he had said.

"He said they had scattered complaints about the vitamins not arriving on time. So I asked if anyone who had gotten the vitamins had actually lost weight. And he didn't know. Apparently this was too subtle a distinction for him to make. Even at $3.80 cents per minute."

At this point I got a little overheated. "Products are the language of our times. They're how we tell each other that we care and obviously we don't." Then Wordsworth kicked in.

"Getting and spending we lay waste our powers," I said.

"Little we see in nature that is ours," I said.

"We have given our hearts away, a sordid boon!"

———————————

The program is slated to air right before the Oscars. Probably they'll cut the poetry. I pray God they don't edit out my closing line.

"You know, Barbara, I'm not actually a murderer," I told her. "I just play one on TV."

This was my first television interview, and a lot of other networks had tried to book me. The NBC producer seemed the most sympathetic. "Listen, Noel, we want you to talk about your pain," he said. Pain? But I'm as happy as a pig in shit.

EDITORIAL PREFACE

At the end of the war, when he was living on cream cakes in his bunker under the Berlin Chancellery, Adolf Hitler concluded that he had not been ruthless enough. Reduced largely to the company of his dog, Blondi, the Fuehrer spoke with Goebbels about a growing admiration for Stalin. Stalin had extirpated the Russian nobility. In the spring of 1945, Hitler felt that he had been mistaken in letting some German aristocrats survive. On the

27th of April, three days before he killed himself, according to Paul John-son in *Modern Times*, Hitler wrote, "Afterward you rue the fact that you've been so kind."

Although our subject is certainly not the great villain that Hitler was, the two men are similar in that they share a very considerable talent for self-delusion. Neither man suffered any remorse.

Thirty-four people, including a stunning seven-year-old chess prodigy named Jennifer Solotof, had been killed by the time Noel Hammersmith was apprehended. The girl died in her mother's arms, after her carotid artery was sliced in the blast of a bomb set off in the Customer Service department at Crazy Eddie's, which was then located on Central Avenue in Yonkers, New York.

Jennifer was the victim most frequently used to illustrate stories about the Wordsworth Bomber, which was what they began to call him long before they had any idea who he was. The story's signature illustra-tion was two pictures often presented side by side. The first showed Jen-nifer smiling brilliantly and holding up a trophy she'd won at a competition held at the Plaza in Manhattan. The other was a shot of the same girl lying limp in her mother's arms in the wreckage of the electronics store. In the background was a large white poster with the words "You Have to Be Insane" emblazoned across it in red.

When the FBI connected the later bombings with others that had taken place as early as 1984, the case drew national attention. Afterward there was a good deal of finger wagging about how Noel escaped even being a suspect. The classic sociopath is a recluse. Hammersmith was not a recluse. He'd lived in Bedford Hills, he'd worked in Manhattan. He once actually told a psychiatrist that he was considering killing people in order to become famous.

So much attention has been paid to this sad story that questions have been raised about the judgment of publishers and newspeople in glorifying the criminal protagonist. For man—the lonely animal—attention of any sort can seem a reward, and even an encouragement.

For this reason, we would like to state at the outset that we, the edi-tors of this book, have no admiration for our subject. We are fascinated—who has not been fascinated by this odd, and gruesome story? We do not approve. We abhor a process that transfigures the most despicable criminal into a celebrity.

Nor are we convinced by Hammersmith's protestations of innocence. Nobody in jail is ever guilty. The worst criminals have the worst cases of self-delusion. When David Berkowitz (aka Son of Sam) was apprehended in August of 1977 and charged with six murders and seven woundings, he maintained that he was following instructions given to him by his Labrador retriever. Hammersmith didn't own a pet, but he too has passed the buck. The crimes for which he was charged were committed, he seems to think, by a phantom writer, a man who took the name of Che Guevara.

According to Dr. Cleo Santarelli, Hammersmith's psychiatrist—and a woman without whose help this book could not have been written—it is inevitable that a certain type of highly pious individual will first suppress and then externalize his less acceptable impulses. "It is a commonplace," she explained, "for a husband to blame his wife and children when he regrets the dull sameness of his existence. In the more dramatically pathological states, an entirely invented character shoulders the burden."

We can all understand, I am sure, how disappointing it must have been to discover that Brooks Brothers no longer carried a favorite style of shirt, or that mail order products that arrived unbidden were also broken, and therefore not returnable. Nobody likes to get buffaloed by a crooked purveyor of diet pills. Especially if one has a legitimate weight problem.

And yet, to quote Barbara Walters, most of us do not take the law into our own hands. We do not plant bombs in Grand Central Station on Christmas Eve. Most of us lack the grandiosity required to imagine, as our subject did, that our personal wrath is the concern of a national political party, the Know-Nothings, nor would the average man suppose his grievances sufficient to detonate the nuclear reactor at Indian Point in northern Westchester.

There are stories circulating now in the less reliable press that accept Hammersmith's version. And it is true that several articles have appeared in *Soldier of Fortune* magazine under the byline Che Guevara, but these were written by a number of different individuals, none of whom conform in any way to the person Hammersmith has described. Detective

Tom Janus, the man who headed the investigation that ultimately led to the arrest of Hammersmith, has assured us repeatedly that Noel was "our first and only suspect."

In this, *The Compleat Wordsworth Bomber,* the most thorough work to date, the perspective provided by the journals will be widened with the addition of letters `set in Typewriter MT` written to Hammersmith's close friend, the lawyer, Fulton Halloway; to Noel's sister; and to various manufacturers who had offended the subject's perhaps too finely honed sensibilities. In response to the immense interest generated by the case, the editors have taken it upon themselves to depose more than 300 corroboratory sources. The data pulled from the transcriptions in Franklin Gothic will be used to buttress the narrative, most of which is still revealed in the killer's own words. Hammersmith's journals will be set in Revival 555 Semibold.

The suspect went to see Dr. Cleo Santarelli in February of 1984. He wrote about it in his journal. This journal has been published in thirty-six countries with titles variously translated from that chosen by Knopf: *The Diaries of the Wordsworth Bomber.* Sections of that document were used in the scripting of *The Customer Is Always Right,* a four-part miniseries on NBC in which the Noel Hammersmith character was played "charmingly," according to *Entertainment Weekly,* by Don Johnson.

For the purposes of our study, the psychiatrist seems a good place to start, right at the limit of rational understanding. Noel was working then at Acropolis, a publishing firm once famous for having brought Kafka to America, but which has since been absorbed by Pretty Kitty, Inc., a multinational real estate and entertainment conglomerate that had started as a purveyor of cat food and cat toiletries. When Hammersmith saw the psychiatrist, the firm was still independent and had the generous benefits of a private and paternalistic employer.

1

MURDERERS ARE OAFS

THURSDAY, FEBRUARY 9, 1984. I weigh 189 lbs. I'm fat and the pen ($3.95) I had left in the jacket pocket of my Paul Stuart suit has leaked all down the lining. So naturally, I'm depressed. But this time, I'm going to do something about it. Acropolis may not be a first-rate publisher, but it does have a first-rate health plan, and so people like me, people like myself, functioning melancholiacs, can see a psychiatrist once a week at $100 an hour. Which I am now doing. I got the woman's name from Human Resources, phoned this morning and saw the doctor this afternoon. This little flower aims to bloom. Speaking of blooming, my shrink won't talk about diet.

"This is NOT Weight Watchers," she said, and she said it disdainfully. Disdain is what I get from attractive women. Doctor Santarelli is an attractive woman. She was wearing black cowboy boots with white stitching, and a long suede skirt, suitable for riding sidesaddle. Paint a powder smudge on her pale white cheek and she might have stepped out of a TV western. She had everything but the carbine.

No wedding band. But, then, aren't they supposed to hide their wedding rings for therapy? That way the patient is free to imagine that the doctor is really his mother. Or his lover. Or both. You're also supposed to pretend that the psychiatrist would still care about you for no money. Which is way too much heavy lifting for this dwarfish imagination.

Doctor Santarelli does seem to think the journal is a good idea. Especially since I'm having so much trouble with my memory. She wants me to spice the entries with current events. "Place yourself in the exterior world," she says.

I told her about my memory lapses. "I lose whole days," I told her.

She wanted to know if I'd seen a "real doctor" (her phrase), an internist or a neurologist. I told her that I had been in an automobile accident once, several years ago, and had hit my head, but that afterwards I'd been thoroughly checked. "I seem to be able to function adequately at my job," I said. "I do what's expected of me. It's just that afterward I can't always bring it to mind."

"And what is it about the disability that concerns you the most?"

"The bottom line is that I can't recall what I've eaten. I don't know if I had one bagel with two foil units of cream cheese, or two bagels with one foil unit of cream cheese."

"You can write that down, too," she said. "If you want."

"I might. If I can remember what to write down."

"Write down whatever you remember," she said.

"Do you want me to read my journal here?" I asked. "Or you could read it yourself."

"If you'd like. Not all of it necessarily," she added, quickly. Ever notice how loath people are to read anything longer than their own horoscope? Not a good sign for those of us in publishing. In any case, the doctor expects that the very process of keeping a diary will be therapeutic. She expects that I will get to know myself. "Find out what you need from life."

I told her that was simple. "I know what I need from life."

"And what do you need from life then?"

"I want to be beloved of women. Beloved of many beautiful women. I don't want them to get tired of me either. I want the women always to feel the way they do when we've just met. Or if she's married to a brute."

Cleo didn't look pleased. "This is not a joke," she said.

"And I'm not joking," I said.

"Okay," she said. "Anything else?"

"Thin. It's difficult to get a lot of beautiful women to love you if you're plump," I said.

"You've already mentioned that you want to reduce," she said, and she said it quite sourly.

"And tall," I said. "I'd also like to be tall." This last remark to the psychiatrist was meant to get a laugh. When it failed to do so, I was disappointed but not surprised. I've never yet met a therapist who hadn't had the laugh organ removed. True mental health, apparently, will be the death of humor.

"Is that all you want?" she asked.

"Well, actually there's more," I said, prepared now to horrify my audience.

"Yes?"

"You want to know what I'd really like?"

"Yes, of course," she said, although she was already beginning to sound bored.

"What I'd REALLY like is to be famous."

"Famous?" she asked, as if she'd never heard anything so rude, as if *penis* would have been a better word. Penis envy was something she'd been trained to deal with. Envy envy was not.

"That's right. I want to be a household name."

"Like the president, or more like a movie star?"

"Is there a difference?" I asked.

The doctor shrugged. "I suppose Ronald Reagan confuses the issue. Not all U.S. presidents were movie stars."

"More like a movie star then," I said. "I don't actually have a national platform all thought out. I want to be a sort of modern Buddha, sit somewhere quiet and read my clips." Here she started to take notes, which I considered a good sign. At least I had her attention. "I want somebody to tell my story.

Most lives aren't a tragedy, you know. Most lives aren't recorded at all."

"So you want to be on *Sixty Minutes?*" she said. "Or *Larry King Live?*" and at this point she almost smirked. I don't believe they're allowed to smirk. Not while on duty.

"Or the *CBS Evening News,*" I said. "Any in-depth interview on any news show would be a start as long as it isn't one of those neighborhood cable programs. You know, where they have the village board and advertisements for the Acme Body Shop. Cable is almost as banal as life. I want drama in my episode. I suppose I could also be written up in a best-selling book. Nonfiction. With myself as the hero, protagonist. Then I'd end up on the *Today Show.* I will not go gently into the good night of anonymity. I'm with Mrs. Willy Loman on this: Attention must be paid."

At this point the doctor tried to regain control of the session. "Don't you think that all this is an attempt to make up for something simple, something that you might be able to discover in your own character?"

"Fuck no!" I said, and that made her flinch. She has a fetching little flinch. "Famous people don't necessarily have fully realized personalities," I pointed out. "We often hear about how needy Elizabeth Taylor is, or how sad and lonely Marilyn Monroe was. Monroe actually died with the telephone in her hand. But now I'm off the track. The main point here is that we care about these people. We love them more than we love our own husbands and children."

Cleo scratched her left eyebrow with her left forefinger and sighed noisily. I guess they're allowed to sigh. She was already beginning to think of me as a difficult case, a big, fat problem. "Do you have any clear idea how you might go about getting this attention?"

"I think so."

"Really?" she asked, displaying, I thought, just a little too much surprise.

"Well," I said, and cleared my throat. "I am a creative person. I have a play in me. I think any play I wrote would be special and unique. Something like Edward Albee's *The Zoo Story,* or else *The Death of a Salesman.* Something sad, specific, and universal. Then I could be Arthur Miller, marry Marilyn Monroe."

Now Cleo was openly looking at her watch. A Timex. Takes a licking and keeps on ticking. She was checking to make sure it hadn't stopped. We complain a lot about the time famine, but time isn't only a shortage, it's also a protection. Cleo hoped she was running out of time. Clearly she was running out of patience. "What if playwriting fails?" she asked, and you just knew she thought it would.

"There's nothing about my being fat that means I can't write," I said. "Norman Mailer is plump. Dickens was chubby. G. K. Chesterton was obese. There's no correlation."

Cleo wasn't shocked by this. "I didn't think there was any correlation," she said. "I only wondered if you had another plan. In case the play doesn't win a Tony."

"I suppose I could murder somebody," I said. "I suppose I could murder a lot of people. It takes courage to write a play, talent and money to get it produced. Murderers are oafs."

2

SELFISH!

SELFISH! SELFISH!

IT'S EVENING NOW. I'm at home in Bedford Hills. Alone, alone in perfect solitude. Henry David Thoreau never met a companion as companionable as solitude. So why does it feel like a knife at my throat? When I'm alone, I'm really alone. When I'm alone I barely exist. Sigh. To get a letter, write a letter: Eaton Paper.

```
110 East End Avenue
New York, New York 10028

Dear Kat,

    How is my little sister? I'm fucked. Or not
fucked. Depending on how you want to state it.
Either way it's damn quiet around here. Remember
Ginny? She's gone. This makes seven girls who
have abandoned me so far. Could so many beau-
tiful women all be wrong? Probably not. Ginny up
and vamoosed. Vanished. Fled to Los Angeles.
Plans to join an artists' commune. Paint her
little heart out. Escape the bourgeoisie.
    Didn't Mencken call it the Booboisie? Well,
I'm certainly a member in good standing. Morn-
```

ings, you'll find me on the platform of the
railroad station in Bedford Hills. Dressed as if
to take communion, I listen for the coming of
the 7:52. On this I journey to Manhattan,
dozing, reading the Times or a manuscript. At
noon I go to the Vanderbilt YMCA, change, run
two and a half joyless miles up the East River
and two and a half miles back. Also joyless. I
shower, resume my suit, and return to the
offices of Acropolis, Inc. Coming home after
work, I look like every other white-collar
drudge on the late rattler. Which is to say, not
very well. Which is to say, the walking dead.
Man on a string.

I thought there must be a word for my condition and so fished out The Synonym Finder
(Rodale Press Inc.) This was a Valentine's Day
gift from Ginny. "Your chickadee. Your lovey
dovey," she wrote on the inside cover. "Forever
XXX OOO." It turns out there is a word. There
are several: "Lonely, lonesome, forlorn, bereft,
forsaken; abandoned, deserted, derelict, desolate, out in the cold."

I'm all alone on an increasingly crowded and
dehumanized planet. If I had a fortune, I'd give
it all to Planned Parenthood. There are too
damned many of us. So why can't I find a single
woman who will stick?

Freud said we were supposed to succeed in
love and work. You've heard about the love part.
The work part isn't going all that well either.

Life at The Necropolis, Inc. publishing house
continues to occupy, but not really to engage,
my intelligence. Although I did get a proposal
about foreign terrorists who are supposed to set

off a bomb in Grand Central Terminal. This
piqued my interest on account of Grand Central
Terminal is where Zaro's is, and Zaro's is where
I get my coffee.

I was going to write a play. I was going to
master the harmonica. Instead I lie on my bed
and listen to the refrigerator cycling on and
off. Rummmmm, whisssss whissssss. I consider the
statistics: Single males die young.

One of the much advertised "features" of the
Lord & Lady Ampleworth Apartments is the wooden
floors. I never noticed them before, but
suddenly this one-bedroom unit has acres of
naked board. Walk around and the place echoes
like an empty gymnasium. Is it a whole new life
I need, or only carpeting?

Ginny left a bra in the bathroom. I've kept
it there, over the bar that holds the shower
curtain. It's white, an ordinary brassiere. A
glimpse of this innocent piece of underwear is
enough to take my breath away. Once I actually
surprised myself with a little sob.

Love,
Bro

P.S. Call. Write. Come. Your brother is addicted
to love, addicted to coffee, addicted to food.
Addicted to running. And goes nowhere. And fears
a sprained ankle above all else.

Possession is nine-tenths of the law and Ginny had taken possession of
most of what she and Noel had had in common. "I had the U-Haul," she
explained, cheerfully, when asked about it later. "Seemed silly not to fill it
up." She'd taken the last of the coffee, the last of the milk, the last of the

toilet paper. Saturday morning found Noel in a blue funk, in the line of cars in the fire lane waiting to see the doors unlocked at the A & P. It was cold; everybody had their engines going. When the lights in the store went on and the man in the red apron gave the signal, the cars started to peel off to the parking lot.

Sunday. The Polo Green MG directly in front of me stalled. Newly single and therefore newly gallant, I produced my jumper cables. The MG was driven by an enormous blue ski parka with a hood that was trimmed with fun fur. Still, I had a feeling. The second time the parka climbed out of the car, its hood slipped off and revealed something quite small with brilliant red hair, cut short, and green, green eyes. The girl was approximately my age, early thirties, still fresh faced, but with laugh lines coming in. Afterward she insisted on taking my address.

I tried to shrug this off: "My reward is in heaven."

"Maybe, maybe not," she said.

I shrugged again.

"What if you hadn't come along?" she said. "I suppose I'm old-fashioned," she said, "but I still believe in heroes."

My hopes were dashed though when we met again at the register. Green Eyes was buying a six-pack of baby formula.

Now I'm back at the apartment and sad again. Almost paralyzed by the isolation. It's exactly as if Bedford Hills were near the pole and I, freezing, delicate with the cold, eat shoe leather and fill in the last pages of a dead man's journal.

What is the origin of my despair? I've been told that there was a spectacular Ides of March snowstorm on the night that I was delivered. Both parents slept in the hospital, many died on the interstate, schools and businesses were closed. The birthmark on my left shoulder—faded now—was said to have born a remarkable likeness to the globe. My father, a clergyman and therefore credulous by profession, believed the mark to indicate a strong likelihood of world dominion. I was encouraged to read the philosophers, study the oratory in Shakespeare, the lives of

Alexander, Hannibal, and Henry Ford. And after all that preparation, what have I become? "Another Cromwell, guiltless of his country's blood." I languish completely unnoticed in a culture that has celebrated John Hinckley, Mark David Chapman, Gary Mark Gilmore.

Did I miss my cue? Now that I'm alone, I plan to keep a diary. I will study Noel Hammersmith as if he were a stranger, make a science of life. The document will function as notes to a later self. I'll read the record over and I'll learn, learn, learn. Besides which, self-expression is widely believed to be thinning.

This morning I threw out Ginny's houseplants. And the tampons. (Odd that she should take the toilet paper, leave the tampons.) Sorry about this ruthlessness. I am the new, the tame, the practically androgynous helpmate. I've never killed my own supper. I've never even hunted anything more sentient than a bargain. But left to my own devices the masculine reasserts itself, the savagery erupts. I become a sort of one-man *Lord of the Flies*. I go around with naked floors. I waste the tampons, murder the azalea.

I can't bear the idea of having a woman angry at me, any woman. Ginny is still in my head. Shaving, or taking a shower, I hear her speak. It's as if I were a primitive radio that only got one station. Two stations actually, if you count my own weak signal. Ginny's is a pleasant voice, musical, even sexy. "Asshole!" she says. "Selfish! Selfish! Selfish!"

3

THE BOY SAINT

THERE ARE TWO great problems with being fat. Three actually. The first is that your cheaply manufactured belt—what other type is there nowadays?—shows all the holes you've been using, and have been forced to abandon. A record of perfect failure, right there for everybody to see. The second is that you have to keep on buying new clothes. The third, and even more troubling, problem is that one never knows when fat really matters and when fat doesn't matter at all. Nobody ever says, "I won't dance with you because you're fat." Nobody ever says, "You're too chubby to put your hand under my skirt." But when Ginny said I was selfish she might have meant I was fat. Because I'm not all that selfish. And I am all that fat. Besides which, women adore selfish men.

Take Giff. Giff's the handsome, profane, sub-four-hour marathoner I sometimes meet at the Y. Now he sells TV slots to advertisers. He used to be an FBI agent. Even without the law enforcement background, Giff's the sort to turn a woman's head. He's got to be six one or two, with black hair, dark blue eyes, and a square chin. White, even teeth. All this and about as sensitive as a piece of lawn furniture.

Giff's got a new pair of running shoes. Adidas. "They wear like iron," he explains. Yes, but you might as well fasten boards to the bottoms of your feet. I prefer New Balance. Squishy, squashy. Plus made in the USA. I need a fresh set every three months. Someday Giff will need a fresh set of knees.

We ran up the East River Friday, circled the flagpole at Gracie mansion. That's five miles. The night before he'd invited a "friend" to his apartment. They met at a bar. "I knew I liked her," Giff explained, "because her fingernail polish exactly matched her shoes, belt, and pocketbook."

"What color?" I asked.

"Black," Giff said. He and the girl had pizza. Then each other. I'll record our conversation as if I were writing a play. I'll put our names in capital letters, use colons, stage direction wherever possible. I'll get in the habit of being a playwright, strengthen the dramatic muscle.

ME: "What did you have on the pizza?"

GIFF: "Anchovies."

ME: "You like anchovies?"

GIFF: "Hate them. The salt makes the women thirsty. They drink more beer. Which makes them dizzy, or rather it makes them dizzier." Then Giff told me what she wore. (Black jeans, a white cashmere sweater, stiletto heels). What she took off; when she took it off.

ME: "Are stiletto heels always a good sign?"

GIFF: "Except on a whore. Otherwise they're always a good sign."

ME: "Are you in love?"

GIFF: "No."

ME: "Is she in love?"

GIFF: "Christ, I hope not. My wife would be so annoyed."

Since they didn't work together and there was no consanguinity, Noel and Giff could be wonderfully candid. The men spoke freely of masturbation, money troubles, and even despair. Noel told his psychiatrist that he withheld only one piece of information, a secret that he was certain would end the friendship. This was that he, Noel, had never cheated on a woman.

Any woman. Not once. "Do you often consider probity a social handicap?" she'd asked. "Yup," he said. "That's right."

The boy saint. That's what his father used to call him, although it wasn't exactly a compliment. We learned from Noel's psychiatrist that the older man had only struck his son once. This was when Noel grabbed the steering wheel and made the priest pull over so that they could check on the condition of a squirrel that had been hit by the station wagon in front of them. The road had no shoulder. There had been a pickup truck immediately behind the Hammersmith family sedan. The gesture had very nearly cost both of them their lives.

"I love your intentions, Noel," his father is reported to have said afterward, still clutching the steering wheel, still panting with fear, "but you've got to be practical, live in the world."

It was his parents' tragic and notorious death that drew me to Noel in the first place, Ginny told us. "A girl likes a sad story," she said. So for a while there she tolerated his yearning for righteousness. Although just barely. "If you weren't so kind, you'd be a prig," she said. Every Saturday morning, Noel would write a letter to the little boy in Ecuador, whom he was supporting at $15.35 a month. Pedro. That was his actual name. When Ginny and Noel were first together, he used always to bring twice the money or tokens needed and pay for the car behind them. "Someday this will start a chain," he said.

"I'm doing it because I adore you," he said. "We'll call it the Ginny chain." Then one evening crossing into Manhattan, Noel let the second token slip through his fingers. He started to search frantically on the floor. The collector was waving madly at him to drive through. The man behind him, the one whose toll he was trying to pay, started in on the horn.

"I wonder," Ginny said afterward, "were all the saints this difficult to get along with?"

"They lived alone," Noel said. "Mostly they lived alone."

Ginny was an artist, a painter. She rendered the faces and naked tor- sos of famous killers. She painted them in oil (never acrylic) and larger than life. Noel was allowed to stretch the canvas beforehand and apply gesso. Sometimes she posed him, used a detail from an arm or shoulder. Mostly, she worked from a cardboard carton filled with pictures and clip- pings. The carton was gone. All of the canvases were gone as well on that Friday when Noel came back from work expecting supper. Plus two old Brooks Brothers shirts she'd been using as smocks. These were the last of Noel's father's shirts.

She'd taken the stereo too, of course (a JVC). And the TV (a twelve- inch Sony). Noel missed her terribly, but he also remembered that she had kept the stereo on full blast during the day, the TV at night. She told people this blocked the conscious channels of her mind, freed her for cre- ation. He had to shout at the top of his lungs to be heard in his own small apartment. "Living here is like living under a waterfall," he said in one of his rare outbursts. There was never any silence. There was hardly any air either, Noel told his doctor. We loved each other deeply, he said. We didn't like each other at all.

"Love is a curse, a spell they cast and the first article of what will soon become an endless Bill of Rights," Noel told Giff as they ran up the East River in a drilling rain. "When a woman says she loves you, it's like she's detonated the neutron bomb. Afterward all the buildings look the same, all the people are dead."

"That's your own fault," Giff had shouted back. "You should never fuck a woman who loves you. I never do."

"That's because you're handsome," said Noel. "I'm fat. Nobody this fat ever gets fucked without first being passionately in love."

"It's been eight days now since Ginny left," he confided, wiping the rain off his face with the back of his hand. "Already I've forgotten everything but the way her body smelled."

Fulton Basque Holloway
Holloway, Holloway & Stone
230 Benefit Street
Providence, Rhode Island 02903

Dear Tony:

Writer one to writer two. Do you hear me? Are
you out there? Are you finishing your novel? Are
you reaching for greatness? Bringing order to a
random universe? Or are you only imagining
fucking my sister?

Fuck my sister. Marry my sister. See if I
care. Yes, I know just how pretty she is. And a
voice so compelling they used her for radio
advertising. She's also treacherous. Quite aside
from the fact that she's married. As are you.
How is sweet Polly these day? Is Evan playing
hockey again this year?

But no, I won't set you up. Write her a
letter yourself, Mr. Slowpen. The address is in
the Manhattan directory. Under beautiful but
deadly. Just kidding. A person with your connections ought to be able to get his hands on a
Manhattan phone book.

Of course she says she's interested in your
writing. She knows that's your tender point. And
has grabbed it. Take it from me, she's not
interested in your writing. How could she be?
You've never written anything. She's interested
in your money. And the novelty. A lawyer. She
hasn't had a lawyer yet. The doctor is beginning
to bore her.

Speaking of letters, you now owe me three.
Four and I'll find some other failed novelist to
confide in. You don't think they're out there?
Postcards from your secretary don't count.

Love,
No

P.S. Tell Polly I still run five miles a day,
every day. And sometimes, on a quiet night, like
tonight, I still miss her. Does she remember me
at all? The boy saint.

4

ADAPT OR DIE

MONDAY, FEBRUARY 13, 1984. I knocked my shatterproof alarm clock off the bedside table this morning, attempting the snooze button, and it shattered. I'm tired of everything falling apart. But then I'm also just tired. Except right after my third cup of coffee. I weigh 189 lbs. First Great Reason for Thinness: If you're hungry, you won't be so tired. You'll need to be alert. In case something to eat walks by.

Mario Cuomo says that work is a prayer. Certainly it's a distraction.

I pray on the 37th floor of the Pan Am Building, high up in the most hated skyscraper in the most hated city in America. Pieces of paper often float up in the canyon between this building and the one across 45th Street, and flutter there, suspended at a great height. I would like to open my window and grab one of these notes. The window is sealed. The entire building is sealed. Rather like a prison. I take to the altitude and enjoy peering down on the street below, as if I were a god, or a giant. Not everybody does take to the altitude. When I started as an editorial assistant, the firm also hired another young man who got dizzy and had nosebleeds. He couldn't bear the terrarium. "Inhuman," he called it. "I feel like somebody's pet gerbil," he said and quit.

There's a commotion going on down the hall. They're installing a splendid bank of filing cabinets for the business type who just moved up from 36. Tollah is his name. Something Tollah. Bill Tollah? Alan Tollah? He flew helicopters in Vietnam. He's a graduate of the Dale Carnegie University of Unrealistic Expectations and has coal black eyebrows and prematurely gray hair. Tollah arrived with his own secretary. She arrived with an English accent. Pip, pip. Archer Peabody, the publisher, told us Tollah's moving up here to study our technique and culture. "He needs to understand the delicate editorial processes." Archer Peabody is lying. Tollah's here to find out what we're doing wrong.

It's not what we're doing wrong, it's that we're the wrong people. In the wrong place. At the wrong time.

I must exclude Amelia, the department secretary. She has nothing to do with books and would as lief work for Josef Mengele as for me. The rest of us do care. We manufacture carriages in a world of fossil fuel. We all of us read a book once and were impressed. The world advanced and we stayed in that moment, alone with a book.

Start with me, fat, foolish and with a strangely exaggerated sense of destiny. Then take Nancy. Campbell calls her the Westinghouse. Because she looks just like a refrigerator. She has her hair in a youthful page boy and wears a blue blazer with a crest. You might easily mistake her for the family fridge, or else the world's oldest, fattest English schoolboy. Also, if you can believe this, she's vain.

She was here when I came. And thinks me an interloper. A carpetbagger. She met me in the hall on one of my first days of service. "Even a rat will fight when cornered," she said. Not exactly Welcome Wagon. We get along. By avoiding each other.

Nobody healthy would pick this business at this time in history. Now that we've been moved to the sideshow. We're the grotesque in the circus that is the world of entertainment: the stuffed mermaid, the bearded lady, the cow with five legs.

Campbell's an old pro. He might actually be a decent editor, if he did any editing anymore, but he doesn't do any editing anymore.

All headed by Archer Peabody. I have worked under the man for years, and still don't know if he's kind, or only distracted. I've never heard a cruel word cross his lips. He graduated from Yale. I can't give you the year, but it must have been before the people in New Haven recognized the utility of a spoken language. Archer Peabody won't talk. It's always as if we've just come out of a football huddle. He makes encouraging grunting noises and pats us on the back. You rarely hear him string three words together. Which would be OK if we weren't in publishing. Words being our bread and butter.

He used to be the *capo de tuti capi*, but now he's not. Now we've got Tollah, a sort of CEO, a man who seems to have gotten his personality out of a self-help book.

Napoleon said, "I have no sense of the ridiculous. Power is never ridiculous." And so Tollah isn't ridiculous. Campbell hates Tollah. Campbell says that the great secret of the modern American businessman is that he's not good at business. "We've heard he's ruthless, cares nothing for aesthetics, ethics, or even for the bottom line, if you go more than two fiscal years. We know he came from sales and not from production. They hop from industry to industry and so often aren't even familiar with their own product line. All of this is public knowledge. What we haven't yet figured out is that these people are not just bad for business, they're bad at business."

The new guy hasn't actually done much yet. Except he came up with a slogan. He found out how small we are, and now after the title of the company he's put a colon, and the phrase: the best little publishing house in America. It's not true, of course, not by a long shot, but it has a ring to it.

Outside of sloganeering, the one thing the new breed does understand is status. Which is why they're very careful about their neckties and are always building bigger offices for themselves. Tollah is building a bigger office for himself. It's in the corner and big enough for badminton. For a month now I've been meeting workmen in the toilet. They wear white coveralls and carry silver lunch boxes. Often they smoke.

Before my run today I stopped to see what the coveralls had wrought. Ms. BBC was at lunch, or having her legs waxed. I was able to walk right in, violate the sanctuary. Apparently it's not alarmed. Although there is a TV. And a VCR. Tollah's got a gigantic wooden desk with two brass lamps. A Lucite cube with pictures of the obligatory loved ones. There seems to be a wife in the picture, and two boys. On the leather sofa there's an embroidered pillow. Says "Adapt or Die."

5

WHAT THOSE PEOPLE
DID FOR GOD

Monday, Feb. 13, 1984

President
Brooks Brothers
346 Madison Avenue
New York, N.Y. 10017

To Whom It May Concern:

Feeling somewhat rootless, I went to your
flagship store on Madison Avenue this afternoon
to buy shirts and was frightfully dismayed to
discover that you have discontinued the Brooks
Brothers Blue.

My father was a minister in the Episcopalian
Church and fought the introduction of the new
Book of Common Prayer. He and I used to make
regular pilgrimages to your store. We knew, of
course, that generals Grant and Sherman wore
Brooks suits. We'd been to the Ford Theater in
Washington, D.C. and had seen the frock coat
from Brooks which they cut off Abraham Lincoln,

after he was shot in the head. I don't suppose
it was a comfortable coat. The flannels I wore
as a boy were excruciating. It was a family joke
that my Sunday clothes fit so poorly that you
could have opened fire with a revolver, hit the
suit six times, and left me unscathed. And yet
our hilarity must not be mistaken for irrever-
ence. I wasn't a Brooks man, but I certainly
meant to be one. Your store represented a
respectability that was worth striving for.

Plus there was room in the clothing for a
full-sized man, any sized man. The suits fit
everybody--or should I say didn't fit every-
body--to the same degree.

Now you've drawn in all your seams. Handsome,
slender men look better. The rest of us look
horrid. You have put a pocket on the Brooks
Brothers Blue, which shirt lacked a pocket in
the same way that The New York Times lacks
comics.

Reluctantly yours,
Noel Hammersmith

From Brooks and unburdened by packages Noel had gone down into
Grand Central Terminal to the B. Dalton and bought *Country & Blues Harmonica for the Totally Hopeless/From the People Who Brought You Jug-
gling for the Complete Klutz*. At home that evening he spent half an hour
trying to master "The Marine Hymn." Then 4C began to bang on the ceiling. Noel lived in 3C. 4C (aka Mrs. Whiting) was a widow and apparently
not a music lover.

Noel was in the middle of his fifteenth reading of *The Tale of Two*

Cities, but when he got into bed, he turned instead to *The Journals of Henry David Thoreau.* We can't be absolutely certain what page he was on that night, but it was at about this time that he marked the following passage: "The Indian stands free and unconstrained in Nature, is her inhabitant and not her guest, and wears her easily and gracefully. But the civilized man has the habits of the house. His house is a prison."

Tuesday, February 14, 1984. 9 A.M. In office. My elaborate desk chair with special padded lumbar support is broken. I reclined in it two days ago. The chair has been reclining ever since. I've got a call into maintenance. I know I phoned maintenance because I wrote it down. I need to write things down. I keep flashing in and out of focus. I'm here and determined not to eat anything. Suddenly, twenty-four hours have passed. I seem to have eaten. I seem to have eaten well. Two days ago I woke up in a nest of empty Mounds wrappers. Days vanish. It's as if I were sleepwalking, only nobody else notices. My dream life has slopped over into the waking world. My life—as I know it—is banal. Is it possible I'm having thrilling adventures that I just can't remember? How else would I have gotten so hungry?

The Second Great Reason for Thinness. An article by Jane Brody from *The New York Times.* Headline: "Eating Less May Be the Key to Living Beyond 100 Years." Opening paragraph: "In searching for ways to extend the human life span and to ward off the diseases of old age, some scientists find themselves focusing not on enhancing diet but rather on limiting it."

Almost noon. It looks as if I am skipping lunch.

Campbell knocked once on my door and opened it.

"No?"

"Yes."

"Sushi?"

"No."

"A no from No," Campbell said and vanished before I could reconsider. Campbell is a big man but quick and agile, like a trained bear.

I earned the nickname in high school, after having displayed an extreme reluctance to be called upon in class.

TEACHER: "Mr. Hammersmith. Would you care to comment on the issues which led to hostilities between England and the American Colonies?"

ME: "No."

TEACHER: "Would you care to give the class one example of a disagreement between the British home government and the American Colonies?"

ME: "No."

TEACHER: "Would you care then to address the class on any subject even obliquely related to American history?"

ME: "No."

So they call me No. It's a little negative, or that's what Campbell said when we first became friends. It's also simple and to the point. A woman who will says, "Yes, No," to me, or "No, Yes." "Yes! Yes!" would be better I suppose, but then I can't figure out what Yes would be short for.

10:57 P.M. I weigh 189 lbs. on the bathroom scale. I'm five foot eleven inches tall. Large frame. Or that's what I tell myself. A lard Ass. A tubaluba.

When our subject came home the following night there were three packages outside his door. According to his neighbor, a Mrs. Whiting in 4C, who met him in the hall, he was absurdly thrilled. Noel showed his upstairs neighbor his gifts. He got a chess set in which the men were figures from the Civil War. Plus a necktie with donkeys on it and a double-chocolate chocolate cake.

Evening alone. It must be Green Eyes shipping me the gifts. The formula must be for somebody else's baby.

Thursday night in Bedford Hills. The second round. Federal Express delivered Aunt Milly's All-Natural Five Pound Strawberry Cheesecake. Which I walked immediately to the incinerator.

We didn't touch. I would remember if we had touched. But after the car started, after her little engine roared to life, our eyes did lock. It was only a second, less than a second, but there was no denying it: our eyes did lock: Positive to positive, negative to ground.

Saturday morning, Noel rushed down to the A & P. No Green Eyes. He came home and found the United Parcel man in the lobby. Noel signed for a box of Belgian chocolates and a set of knives, the sort that cut through steel. Walking the chocolates to the incinerator, he concluded that all these gifts must have cost a fortune. "She's probably an heiress," he wrote in his journal. "She's afraid I'll be too proud to accept her money."

That Sunday he failed to go to church. Instead he took an eleven-mile run, up through Katonah and around the reservoirs. After his shower, our sources indicate that Hammersmith put on his favorite album: *Johnny Cash in Concert at Folsom Prison*. He listened to the music while he swept the floor of his small and carpetless apartment. "I shot a man in Reno, just to watch him die." Behind the deep, masculine voice of Cash, Noel could hear the prisoners roar with glee. Like the crashing of surf against a rockbound coast. "When I was just a small boy, my momma told

me, son, always be a good boy, don't ever play with guns. Well I shot a
man in Reno, just to watch him die."

Monday, Noel's ancient Chevy (the heartbeat of America) wouldn't turn
over. He called the garage and arranged for a mechanic to come up and
examine the car. Then he took a cab to the station. He took a cab home.
The mechanic had fixed the car and left him a bill for $135. His sister,
Katherine, remembers phoning Noel at about this time and reports that
he sounded fine, if slightly disoriented. Tuesday went by in a flash. He had
no recollection of it. No proof that he'd existed at all that day. Wednesday,
February 22, he got a cowboy hat and Trivial Pursuit. The hat was the
wrong size.

Almost big enough to sleep under. She must consider me a
genius. Either that, or she wants to show me she likes her men
husky. Fat headed. Fat all over. Still, I wish she'd lay off the mer-
chandise altogether and bring her little body over here instead,
wipe my fevered brow.

First thing when we get together, I give her the complete
works of Nathan Pritikin.

Thursday, February 23, Noel's secretary reports his having gotten a call
from the man who wanted to sell a book about terrorists to the best little
publishing house in America. It was quite by accident, according to
Amelia, but she had put her own phone on speaker and had forgotten to
hang up. The caller, who might well have been a friend just kidding
around, had identified himself as Che Guevara. Che was supposed to
have had a doctorate in comparative literature. During the brief conversation she overheard the man also identify himself as a chess prodigy and a
Civil War buff.

"If this was a friend," Amelia said later, "it would have made sense for him to go on about his qualifications and the book he wanted to write, on account of Tollah was spying on people, and Tollah suspected that some editors were abusing their phone privileges by talking to friends during business hours."

"I had planned to come to town soon anyway," the man who identified himself as Che had said. "I need to go to Brooks. Have they cleaned up the mess from the bombing?" Noel said they had reopened. Noel said he believed that the explosion in question was caused by a steam pipe, not a bomb.

"Whatever," the writer said. "I need to go there. Which puts me in town. I thought we might meet."

Noel allowed as how they might meet.

February 1984
110 East End Avenue
New York, New York 10028

Dear Kat,

Yes, I'm still in touch with Tony, but no, he doesn't ask about you. Bill's your husband now. Remember? You're supposed to cleave to him, whatever that means.

Adultery is a sin, right? You told me you were done with that phase of your life.

Meanwhile, my own exemplary existence has gotten so boring, I can't even remember it from day to day. My psychiatrist claims I'm hiding something. Not even she can imagine a grown man with a routine so devoid of meaning. And she's a professional.

There is one bit of excitement. I've got a new writer named Che Guevara. He wants to report on international terrorism. He says we're headed for a new Golgotha. I wonder if he knows that

Golgotha's the place where Christ was crucified?
I still can't figure out if our upbringing is
helpful. What do you get from a thorough knowledge of the Bible? What do you get from a
yearning for righteousness?

I wonder if Che Guevara's his real name.
Couldn't be his real name. It wasn't Che
Guevara's real name. Do you suppose Ernesto is
his real name? Do you suppose he's Hispanic? Do
you suppose he exists at all? I don't care, as
long as he can spell and knows to double space
the manuscript.

Is he credible? How should I know? All
previous writings have gone to Soldier of
Fortune. If we did buy it, Che's work would be
quite the little change of pace. Mostly we
peddle literature, by which I mean novels and
short story collections by writers you've never
heard of. Each has its own title, of course,
pithy and ironic. But if we titled them all
"Whither Me?" nobody would be misled. Not that
many people are misled. The "Whither Mes" don't
sell worth a damn. Diet books are what keep us
afloat. Written by doctors. Fat doctors.

One hundred years ago a distinguished family
would send its least promising, its most suscep-
tible children into the clergy. Nowadays we go
into publishing. I pray we're not doing for
books what those people did for God.

Love,
Bro

6

WHAT A CUNT!

F riday morning Archer Peabody showed up in Noel's office. Peabody was still a good-looking man, poised and charming if apparently uninterested in his work. In fact the publisher was so good-looking that Noel was always surprised to find himself pleased at first, whenever the older man appeared. Archer beamed, came behind Noel's desk, and patted the associate editor on the back. "How's the boy?" he asked. "Terrible, terrible," he said before Noel could speak and pulled a long face. Noel shrugged. "Which boy?" he asked.

"Your son," said Archer. "How's the chemo going?" "I don't have a son," said Noel. Peabody nodded, looked slightly bewildered. "Hmmmm?" he said, then chuffed good-naturedly a couple of times. "And who do I think you are?" the publisher asked, with just the touch of an accusation in the question, as if Noel had practiced to deceive.

"I wouldn't know, sir," said Noel, struggling to keep the acid out of his own voice. Then Peabody spotted the bag of running clothes that Noel kept stashed on the floor behind his desk. "Ah," he said, and chuffed with satisfaction. "Still running every day?" he asked. Noel allowed as how he was still running every day. Archer wondered if that was wise. "I mean carrying all that weight," he said. "Your knees? Your ankles?"

Met Giff in the locker room of the Vanderbilt YMCA.

"Ever want to kill a person?" I asked, as soon as we hit Sutton Place.

GIFF: "Why do you suppose I joined the Bureau?"

ME: "But you quit?"

GIFF: "I quit because they never let me kill the right ones."

We went all the way up to the wire factory. That's four miles out. Neither of us spoke until we'd turned back. Then I told him about the heiress.

GIFF: "What about the other one? The paintress?"

ME: "She left."

GIFF: "Why?"

ME: "She claimed I was addicted to coffee. She said I sweat up the sheets at night."

GIFF (running faster): "Do you sweat up the sheets?"

ME (running harder to keep up): "Yes."

GIFF (over his shoulder): "What?"

ME (coming abreast): "I said yes."

GIFF: "What else?"

ME: "I'm separated from my own feelings. This means I can't believe enough in her art. Which is why she can't believe enough in her art. She needs support. It turns out I'm an essentially ungenerous person."

GIFF: "Does her art suck?"

ME: "I think so."

GIFF: "How long has it been?"

ME: "Two weeks, I guess. I'm miserable. Seems like I've been alone now for an eternity."

GIFF: "You'll recover. It's like a bee sting: first the pain, then the itch, then you can't remember what all the fuss was about."

ME: "What I need now in my life is a larger meaning, something more than a woman to believe in."

We stopped so that I could tie a shoe. "I need a sense of urgency, or rather I need a direction for the sense of urgency I already have."

GIFF: "You're not alone, fella."

We speeded up on the flat, clear stretch of asphalt right beside the East River. We both ran hard for a bit, not speaking.

I'd guess we were breaking an eight-minute mile. Giff isn't quick for a thin man. I'm fast for a fat one.

GIFF (as we slowed to climb the hill you hit between the heliport and the 59th Street Bridge): "That's possible."

ME: "What's possible?"

GIFF: "A larger purpose."

ME: "Is it?"

GIFF: "Sure, sure. But probably you'll go for the common cure."

ME: "And what's that?"

GIFF: "Strange."

ME: "Strange what?"

GIFF: "Strange pussy."

We raced the last mile or so back to the Y and didn't talk again until after the shower. We were sitting across from each other on tin stools in the locker room of the Business Man's Club, pulling on dark socks. Actually, the Business Man's Club is a locker room, a locked locker room with a shower.

GIFF: "Would you give me Ginny's phone number?"

ME: "No."

GIFF: "Do you have herpes?"

ME: "No."

GIFF: "Then give me her phone number."

ME: "No."

GIFF: "Why ever not?"

ME: "I can't believe you asked. What if you started fucking her? How would I feel then?"

GIFF (shrugging): "Flattered?"

ME: "Guess again." I stood up, closed my locker. "Besides, she's living in California."

GIFF: "Lord knows the people in my business never go to California."

I went to the mirror at the end of the room, straightened my collar and tied my necktie.

GIFF: "But you do have her number?"

ME: "Yes."

GIFF: "Which you're not going to share with me?"

"That's right," I said, shrugging on my suit jacket and heading for the door.

"And to think," said Giff, "that that horrid woman had the nerve to call YOU ungenerous. What a cunt!"

7

FUR COAT FOR DOLL
NOT INCLUDED

That Saturday morning Noel made it to the A & P again early. Green Eyes was there. In produce. Squeezing a melon. The baby was enormous. So was the husband. Must have been *his* ski parka. There were introductions all around. She apologized to Noel for not having written.

"I've always wanted to be a writer," she said, "and yet I can't send the simplest note."

"You don't want to be a writer," Noel said.

"Now how would you know that?" she asked, not truculently but with an edge that might simply have been genuine interest.

"Because," said Noel, "I'm an editor."

"Oh really," she said and glanced at her husband. "He's an editor," she said.

The husband nodded.

"Where?" she asked.

"Acropolis," said Noel.

"The best little publishing house in America?" she asked.

Noel shrugged. "More like the best little whorehouse," he said.

"See," she said, turning to her gigantic, deaf husband. "I told you he was modest."

The husband nodded again. "Come on, Fay," he said, took her hand in his and they headed off toward frozen foods.

"Great baby," Noel called after them. "I adore babies."

She flashed a parting smile. Green Eyes had a magnificent smile. Positive to negative, Noel thought, negative to ground. The two parties didn't meet again in the store. She hadn't said anything about the gifts. Noel hadn't said anything about the gifts either.

One hundred and ninety-two pounds seems to be my new set point. That's holding on to the shower door as if my life depended on it. What if I relaxed my grip? How much would I weigh then?

Sunday, February 26, 1984. This morning the shower door pulled out of its hinges. Fortunately, I caught it, and so the glass didn't shatter. The Super has promised to reinstall it next week. In the meantime, I'm going to have to bathe very quickly. Else the bathroom will flood. The hinges are made out of something less durable than tin. The result of our having invented all these new materials during the last thirty years seems to be that everything can be made to break easily, and in ghastly colors. Moondust indeed.

I suppose I'm just in a bad mood. But then this is the best of all possible worlds to be depressed in. The best lack all conviction while the worst are full of passionate intensity. Speaking of which, the U.S. Marines pulled out of Beirut. This is because more than 200 of them were killed in the 1983 bombing. The State Department is chock-full of clever men who wear striped trousers and speak seven languages. They don't make policy, though. Terrorists make policy. Bombs make policy. Sooner or later foreign terrorists are going to come here to set off their bombs. American extremists are already talking about it. There's a party called the Know-Nothings. They want the borders closed. Then they want white supremacy. They speak of setting off bombs themselves, mention targets like the Capitol Building. They talk about armed insurgency. They probably drink Colt 45, wear camouflage pants, and fall asleep in front of the TV.

Speaking of oddballs, I got a call from the Grand Central Bombing fellow. "I wonder if other writers have this problem," Che said. "I hate to sit inside like this. I have to take a day off from work. Which I can do. That's not a problem. My father owns the business. I just hate to sit alone at a keyboard. I seem to disappear. Become almost incorporeal. I feel useless. Do other writers feel useless? Do you ever feel useless?"

"No," I lied. "I don't ever feel useless."

"I see," said Che. "Not even a tiny bit useless. Deluded? Constrained? Claustrophobic?"

"No," I said.

"You're happy in your office?"

"Right," I said.

"I see," said Che. " 'Nuns fret not at their convent's narrow room;

And hermits are contented with their cells.' "

"Exactly," said Noel. " 'And students with their pensive citadels;

Maids at the wheel, the weaver at his loom,

Sit blithe and happy. . . .' That's me. In a nutshell."

Monday. Ran with Giff. The outing was uncharacteristically polite. Giff brought a blond guy along, a weight lifter with a broken nose. The weight lifter had gotten a divorce. His wife wasn't letting him see his daughter.

"Women," said Giff, and shook his head sadly. "How can you trust something that bleeds for seven days and won't die?"

This did not please the weight lifter. He actually bridled. He told Giff that his wife was a fine, young girl. "She just married the wrong man." The weight lifter hated his job. He'd only taken it to support the wife he'd now lost. "I wish I had a career that was not content-free," he said. He was impressed, when he learned that I was in publishing. At Acropolis: The best little publishing house in America. "I used to love to read," he said. "You know that poem," he said. *"Ulysses?"*

I said I knew it.

" 'I hoard and sleep and feed,' " said the weight lifter.

"That's tough," I said.

"You're damn straight it's tough," said the weight lifter.

"You should start again," said Giff. "Start over."

"I'm too old," said the weight lifter.

" 'Old age hath yet his honor and his toil,' " said Giff.

" 'Death closes all; but something ere the end,
Some work of noble note, may yet be done.' "

I told Giff he'd better shut up, or lose his reputation as a blockhead.

"Oh," said Giff. "I didn't know I had a reputation as a blockhead."

"Yup," I said. "International."

Later that afternoon I phoned Giff at his office. "That guy was a downer," I said. "A sad sack."

"I thought you'd like him," said Giff.

"Why the fuck should I do that? Because he knows Alfred, Lord Tennyson."

"No," said Giff. "You should like him, because he isn't kidding himself. And are you going to even ask for that promotion?"

"Yes, but first I'm going to wait until it's late. Always best to call your boss at the end of the day. That way, even if he knows nothing else, he knows you're working late."

"What are you going to say?"

"I've got notes. Want to hear them?"

"No."

"I knew you'd be interested. Here they are:

"1. Establish thankfulness.

"You know how I adore my work, and how thrilled I am to be at Acropolis. It's not just a slogan; we are the best little publishing house in America. A family owned business is a rarity nowadays. So many publishers are being absorbed into corporate conglomerates, or simply sold off for their lists. And working for a legend . . . (I've got to remember to get that in about Archer Peabody being a legend, the man who had tea with Wystan Auden, the man who spilled tomato sauce on Samuel Beckett.)

"2. Without sounding pitiful, show how hurt I have been about the delay.

"There must be some connection between effort and compensation. I'm still an associate editor, but with the responsibilities of a senior staff editor. (Note: Don't seem helpless. Keep your voice in the lower register.)

"Let him talk for as long as he wants. You can't go wrong when somebody else is speaking. Most married men, you just listen to them and they're thankful. That's what Little Sister always says."

"What about your little sister?" said Giff.

"Forget my little sister," I said. "I've got a phone call to make."

But when I called, Peabody was out of town.

I still can't figure out about bagels. I've read that they have 150 calories per. I've also read that they have 350 calories per bagel. And then today, I read that some of them can have 500 calories. Which is it?

Parcel Post arrived at the apartment in Bedford Hills the following evening with a cake, twenty-five pounds of white pistachio nuts, and a box of Godiva chocolates.

"Take the heiress to the Holiday Inn?" Giff asked as soon as we hit Sutton Place on Monday. "You look tired."

ME: "Exactly which heiress are you talking about?"

GIFF: "Take her into the city, then. To the Carlyle? The Pierre?"

ME: "Take who?"

GIFF: "The heiress, stupid. Green Eyes. The little woman."

ME: "I don't know any heiresses."

GIFF: "Sure you do."

ME (running harder): "I do not."

GIFF (keeping up easily): "Now don't go all modest on me. Did she cry out? Did she stuff your underpants with money? Does she have big tits?"

ME: "She doesn't have any tits at all."

GIFF: "That's often true of rich women. I bet she has nice legs. Let me see, an ass like a ripe peach?"

ME: "You don't understand, I'm the heiress."

GIFF: "What?"

ME (slowing down): "Sunday afternoons I pay the bills. I had one from MasterCard. Before she left, Ginny must've copied my number. Plus she knows my Social Security number and date of birth. She sent the presents. She knows I hate Trivial Pursuit. A cowboy hat two sizes too large, a necktie with jackasses on it, sharp knives, fattening cakes."

GIFF: "Clever."

ME: "I never said she was stupid."

GIFF: "How much did it set you back?"

"None of your damn business," I said, and we ran for a mile or so in icy silence. "Besides which, I can return the chess set."

Wednesday, February 29, 1984

President
The War Between the States, Inc.
634 Historic Park
Fort Clearspring, Nebraska 10563

To Whom It May Concern:

    I was given the Amazing Brother-Against-
Brother Deluxe Chess set recently by somebody
with an exaggerated sense of my interest in
chess and in war. When I was packing the gift up
to return it, I found that General Grant's head
had fallen off. I phoned your customer service
number and after spending 15 minutes on hold--
yes, I'm sure of the time, I have a stopwatch.
After spending 15 minutes on hold, I was
informed that if I returned the damaged figure,
he would be replaced.
    Here's the deal: I don't play chess. Would it
be possible for me to return "Brother Against
Brother" for a full refund? Even though Grant is
damaged?

Sincerely,
Noel Hammersmith

Reading in the history booklet that was packed with this expensive and
unwanted toy, Noel came upon and then recorded, Another Great Reason for Thinness: Fighting General Early in the Shenandoah Valley, Phil
Sheridan often sent soldiers behind the Confederate lines. For this particularly tough service, Sheridan didn't like to use men who weighed more
than 138 pounds. He thought the little ones were harder to kill. He was
small himself and by all reports extraordinarily difficult to kill.

Thursday, 11:10 A.M. The new hinges on the shower door seem
to hold my weight. Which was 194 pounds this morning. I
thought sorrow was supposed to make you thin.

    As for Cleo, I've had two sessions this week. The therapist
met me at the door to the clinic for the second visit and said she
tries to start everyone out this way, "like a rocket."

ME: "An ICBM?"

CLEO (leading me into her office and closing the door): "Har, har har."

"So what do you want from all this?" she said, grinning, and waving a hand to include the tin desk, the tin bookcase that held an outdated yellow pages and a children's book titled "Everyone Poops." There was also a *Physicians Desk Reference* for 1969. Which would be great, as long as you got a very old disease.

ME: "I want you to convince me that this is my life."

CLEO: "You don't think this is your life?"

ME: "Well, first there's my memory problem."

CLEO: "But you function adequately. It's a chronic symptom of our time to complain about the failure of memory."

ME: "Yes, but I lose whole days. Like yesterday, for instance, I don't recall yesterday at all. Who knows what I'm doing. Maybe I'm committing serious crimes. Maybe I'm Jack the Ripper."

CLEO (chuckling): "Not bloody likely. But when you do remember, when you are aware of what you're doing and that it's you, don't you feel that it's real then? That it's your life?"

ME: "No."

CLEO: "Explain."

ME: "I'm sure it's not my life."

CLEO (mildly amused): "What is it then?"

ME: "Feels more like a movie. Not a very good one either. I'm wasting the afternoon sitting in a dank auditorium. And all the time I know I should be outside playing ball, or meeting people."

CLEO: "We'd better work on that. The journal should help. Write something down every twenty-four hours and you won't lose whole days anymore. You can read back over the text to persuade yourself that you are flesh and blood."

ME: "Why should I believe what I read in my journal?"

CLEO: "Do you believe what you read in the newspaper?"

ME: "No."

CLEO (smiling vaguely. They are allowed to smile): "I wasn't asking if you believe what Ronald Reagan says. What I meant to ask was whether or not you believed that there is an actual man named Ronald Reagan, and he's the president of the United States."

ME: "I suppose."

CLEO: "Okay, then. You've already started this. Now you should make it policy. Once in a while copy something out of the newspaper into your journal. When you read over it, you'll discover that your life is at least as genuine as are the lives of people in the news."

Which is what I'm now doing. Today, the real-life president denounced his Democratic opponents as cynical professional pessimists. "Will America return to the days of malaise and confusion?" That's what Ronald Reagan wants to know.

There's a plan afoot to cut the federal budget deficit. Also, the Fur Galleria has announced that an authentic Cabbage Patch Doll will be given Free* with any purchase of a fur coat or jacket (adult size)**

On March 6, 7, or 8th.

*Dolls not given for prior purchases.

**Fur coat for doll not included.

8

ARE YOU A COP?

WEDNESDAY, MARCH 7, 1984. Struck out when the bell went off this morning and shattered the second shatterproof alarm clock this year. This one I bought at Crazy Eddie's on Central Avenue for $39.99. I still have the box and receipt.

In more personal news, I weigh 195 lbs. That's up six big ones from the day Ginny left. Quote for the day: The appetite grows by eating.—Rabelais.

Not much world news to speak of. Patrick Buchanan has lost the support of a party called the Know-Nothings. Actually the party name and platform has been resurrected from the nineteenth century. Then they wanted to close the borders, keep out the Irish, Chinese, deport the blacks and Jews. Now they want to close the borders, keep out the Hispanics, Chinese, deport the blacks and Jews. When the police (then mostly Irish) broke up the meetings, the people in the organization would say, "I know nothing." These days many of the actual Know Nothings are Irish. Which is why they don't want to keep out the Irish anymore. They got along with Buchanan for a while. Finally, even he had to have more air. He's a hater, Pat, but not enough of a hater for these people.

Still, if I were a Know Nothing, I wouldn't be unhappy. They got a full-page story in *Time* when Buchanan dumped them. Correction: Almost a full page. There was also a small advertisement for something called Golden Rule Vitamins, Inc. Supposedly you take these pills and the pounds melt away.

Tollah came in to visit me late yesterday evening. That's his actual name. Alan A. Tollah. So naturally Campbell calls him Ayatollah. Ayatollah stalked around my office touching things. Didn't say anything, until he paused at the doorway, right before his exit. Then he made a pistol of his hand, pointed it at my heart. "Bang," he said, smiled and left. Do you suppose Dale Carnegie taught him that?

———————————

Thursday, March 8, 1984. (195 lbs.) It's 10:03 A.M. I'm running my Casio stopwatch to see how long this ordeal called a journal entry takes to complete. I've got a new, black Casio watch. It beeps every half hour. That way I always know what time it is. And that I'm late.

Yesterday afternoon, I spoke again with Che Guevara. Can't get a refund for my War Between The States chess set, so I wondered if he wanted it. Turns out he just recently got one of his own. And you know what? General Grant's head was missing. We got to trading gripes about shoddy manufacturing. I groused about the loss of the Brooks Brothers Blue. He told me he'd just bought a new Swiss army knife, and already the metal tine that keeps the scissors opened has snapped off.

"Brooks is owned by somebody else," he said.

"Everybody is owned by somebody else," I said. "Everybody but us," I said.

"I heard," he said. "The best little publishing house in America."

If I glance back over my shoulder and out the window I can see the Helmsley Building. One of the Helmsley buildings. Some day they'll all be Helmsley buildings. Helmsley or Trump. The Helmsley I see straddles Park Avenue. Come south and there it is, looking like the end of the road. I'm on the other side, gazing north across 45th Street. They've recently touched up the gold work, which looks nifty. I thank Leona for this.

Archer has asked me to scout the upcoming nonfiction of other publishers. I've read 100 pages of *Ten Days to a Successful Memory*. It doesn't seem to be working. For instance, I can't remember who wrote it. Wait a minute, it's not by Joyce Carol Oates. Joyce Carol Oates is the one with the long neck who types ninety words a minute. This one's a doctor, Dr. Carol, Dr. Oates, Dr. Joyce. That's it, Dr. Joyce Brothers. Dr. Joyce Brothers says I shouldn't be "a mood slave." I didn't know I was a mood slave.

I've also got a book that's a collection of transcripts taken from the black boxes of airplanes. I thought it might provide raw material for a play. Call it *The Cockpit of Death*. Or, for a larger audience, *Frequent Flyer to Hell*. The book isn't nearly as thrilling as it sounds, though. Often they suspect nothing. The pilot and copilot are lounging around in their uniforms, chatting up the flight attendants, then: CRASH!!!! End of tape. Even when they do see it coming, death doesn't necessarily make anybody eloquent. "Hot shit!!" That's what one of them said, minutes before being turned into a charcoal briquette. The one interesting fact is that the black box isn't black. It's some sort of easy-to-spot orange.

I had an orange for breakfast. This is good. I also had sugar in my coffee. This is not good. Sugar in both coffees. Sugar in three coffees.

Spent half an hour reading *The New York Times*. I remember nothing outside of an advertisement that asks the question: "Are you a remarkable single person?"

Scheduled to connect with Giff for a run. After all my complaining about loneliness, the world-famous swordsman is finally bringing somebody for me to meet. "Good-looking?" I asked. "I'm not interested in somebody chocked with personality." "A killer," he said. So now I'm going to brush my teeth, shave under my chin. I like to clean up for a killer.

———————

Evening now. At Home Alone. The killer was good-looking all right. Blue eyes. A slender waist. One little problem. Two actually: 1. He doesn't like me. 2. He's a man. A black man. Giff did keep one part of his promise. This date was not chocked with personality. Didn't speak during the run. I didn't even get his name.

This may have had to do with Pig. Pig joined us. Name's actually George. George Peabody (no relation to the publisher). George is what we call him to his face, George or Peas. Behind his back, he's almost universally known as the Pig, or sometimes the BMW. He owns a beamer, of course. The BMW is my age, thirty-something and has one of those sticky-outy noses like a pig. He made a lot of money in the market recently and wants very much to keep it. Pig speaks often of our "punitive tax structure." When Pig begins to talk, he can't easily be stopped. So we ran hard.

Giff finally broke the ice. He'd gotten a parking ticket.

I said, "I hate cops." Giff pulled ahead of the pack. I caught up and we ran alone together for a while. Then the black guy caught up. The BMW was back about thirty or forty feet. I could hear him panting.

ME (to black guy): "I was just saying, I hate cops."

The black guy nodded, but didn't speak.

GIFF: "I was double-parked."

ME: "It's not what they do, it's that they so enjoy it. Policemen are a breed apart. They're a primitive, uncommunicative tribe that somehow got civil service status."

GIFF (looking uneasily at the black guy): "You don't know what you're talking about."

ME: "Sure do. When I was at *The Rockland-Journal News,* it was my job for a while to make the calls for the daily crime blotter. I did it every morning, an hour or so before deadline. If they had a blood drive scheduled, or a softball game, that I'd hear about, or if the PBA was collecting toys for the poor. Otherwise, nothing. Once, on the way to work, I saw a four-car pileup on the Thruway. Two of the cars were burning. I got to the office, called the cops.

ME: "So what's new?"

COP: "Nothing."

ME: "What about the four-car pileup on the Thruway?"

COP: "Oh, that."

GIFF: "So what?"

ME: "They're swine."

GIFF: "Because they want to control the flow of information?"

ME: "Yes. And that's not their job."

GIFF: "So whose job is it, Asshole?"

ME: "I don't know, Asshole. But clearly it's not theirs."

We were heading down Sutton Place at this point, and Pig caught up. His cheeks were crimson with the effort. We slowed the pace and jogged easily back to the Y, heard about the trickle-down economy. The Laffer curve. We all took showers. I was putting on my shirt when I noticed that the black man had a pistol in a brown leather holster, which he'd kept in his locker during the run. He saw me noticing.

ME (embarrassed): "Are you a cop?"

BLACK GUY: "Nope."

9

THE SON OF MAN

When the 7:52 A.M. Express reached New York the main terminal was cordoned off. There were yellow crime-scene ribbons streamered across the entrances and policemen to make certain nobody ducked underneath. Noel is supposed to have asked one of the cops what was going on. "Nothing," he said. So Noel asked a Hispanic in a Zaro's uniform—Zaro's had been evacuated. The man in the Zaro's uniform said there had been a bomb threat. He told Noel he'd seen the police remove one of the large garbage containers. They'd put it on an electric trolley and driven it out to the street. The ones who moved it, he said, were wearing pads and helmets. "They looked like insects," he said. "Black insects."

Noel had to go out into the street himself to get to the Pan Am Building.

According to Amelia, he spent the morning on a proposal for a book to be titled *The Butterscotch Sundae Diet*. The phone in his office rang at noon. "A gentleman is here to see you." That's what Amelia said. She never saw his guest.

3:17 P.M. Che was tall, with a mass of wiry black hair pulled back into an untidy ponytail. He's a businessman. I suppose I have the academic's passion for business, which is to say that in the same instant I both disdain it and find it thrilling. I'm like the loyal husband who has never been to a topless bar; I know I'm too good for such establishments, I know they are dirty and overpriced, maybe even dangerous. And yet I hope and expect that someday, some inferior friend will get me drunk and force me to go.

The walk to the restaurant was uncomfortable, with long silences, expressive, I feared, of mutual distrust.

Once in off the street, I felt less awkward. I'm always cheered to see the freshly laundered tablecloths at Nanni's, and to enter the dark, cool room. The dark, cool, overpriced room. This was an expense account lunch. Che wanted to know what books I had published.

"Mostly diets," I said, buttering some bread.

"But you don't diet yourself?" Che asked, uncertainly.

"It's a failure of belief, really," I said. "Every diet is a sort of toy religion. Every weight loss program is based on an orthodoxy. Eat protein, you'll lose weight. Eat carbohydrates, you'll lose weight. Eat butterscotch sundaes and you'll lose weight."

"Butterscotch sundaes?" Che asked. "How does that work?"

"You eat one butterscotch sundae a day and nothing else."

"What's the rationale behind the butterscotch sundae diet?"

"We eat to satisfy the inner child. The ice cream fills the mouth, in the way a mother's breast might do. The burned or scotched butter represents the disappointments of adult life. That's the theory."

"Is there any validity to that theory?"

"Sure. If you believe it. Believe in any diet, you'll lose weight."

"So why isn't everybody thin?" Che asked.

"People aren't that stupid," I said. "They believe the diet nonsense for a while, then they get hungry. Then they demonstrate their intelligence by gaining back all the weight they've lost."

"Do you have any books out now?" Che asked, putting the white linen napkin in his lap.

I told him about the All-Poison Diet. "We put a powerful emetic into thirty disposable syringes. The set with booklet costs $99.99. The dieter has his spouse, or a friend go through the house and randomly inject eatables. Then he or she is free to browse from anything that might be poison. We have testimonials from people who have lost fifty pounds."

"What goes wrong?"

"Same with all diets. They outsmart themselves. Either they start ordering pizza, or else they spy on the person with the syringe."

"Isn't $100 expensive for a diet?"

"If we could charge $399.99 we'd have even better results. But then somebody else would come out with the *Thrifty Person's All-Poison Diet* and slice the heart out of our market."

"Do they always gain back the weight?" asked Che.

"Usually."

"What then?"

"We sell them another diet book," I said. "My problem is, I can't suspend the disbelief in the first place."

"The books you edit do well?"

"Absolutely!"

Che toyed with his silverware. He waited a minute, then started up again. "You employ other people to write these books?"

"Usually, I do. A doctor is best."

"A thin doctor?" asked Che.

"Sometimes they're thin," I said. "Sometimes they're not thin. You don't need to be thin to write a diet book. You want to write about terrorists. I don't expect you to make the bombs yourself?"

"No," said Che, and smiled broadly. "I suppose not."

At this point the waiter appeared. I ordered a tall glass of grapefruit juice. "It speeds up your metabolism," I explained. Then I ordered the salad with goat cheese and osso buco for the main course. Che said he would drink water, but otherwise have the same meal.

"You could do a book like mine?" Che asked. "Serious non-fiction?"

"Absolutely," I told him. "Back up this story of yours and we can make you a star. We can get you on television."

After this the conversation grew more general, and it was established that I came from upstate New York. I said I'd gone into publishing because my father had been a clergyman. "In the beginning was the word," I said and smiled wearily.

It was also established that Che lived in Connecticut.

"I hope I didn't make you come into town just for this?" I said.

Che said that actually he'd been in the day before and had spent the night at the Waldorf. "My father insists on the Waldorf. He says it's the only hotel in New York." I learned that Che's father owned and operated a construction firm. That Che worked for it. Before that the writer had been employed at a local weekly newspaper. "I was the only Ph.D. on the police beat," he said and smiled bitterly. He told me that it was the contacts he'd made at the paper, and also his knowledge of explosives, picked up on his father's construction sites, that led him to the book project.

By now the main course was being cleared away, and I felt freer to be candid. So I said there had been two bombings recently. "One at the place you and I both got chess sets from and one at Brooks. I feel like Typhoid Mary. But these are not the sort of bombings you fear."

"No," said Che. "My bombers are interested in national policy. America is a large, soft target. We have the worst security in the advanced world," he said, "and the best TV coverage."

Noel stayed late at the office, which by 7 P.M. was empty, even of the cleaning crew, according to Amelia, who had remained in her cubby, quietly. He must have found a directory and the government listing section. It's right there, under Food and Drug Administration. Tollah's door was unlocked. As we reconstruct the incident, the CEO seems to have left his Filofax on his desk. The notebook was green, Florentine leather, with AAT embossed in gold letters. What follows is a transcript of the conversation.

"I have a name I'd like to give you," Noel said when he got through.

"Fine," the voice said, "but first we need some personal information from you."

"Why's that?" asked Noel.

"We get so many tips. We'd like to investigate them all immediately, of course, but that would be impossible. We need some way to determine which are the most pressing."

"Can't I just give you an informal tip? An anonymous tip?"

There followed a mirthless laugh. "I'm afraid not," said the FBI. In this case the FBI was a woman. A black woman, or at least somebody from the South.

"There's this guy you should look into," said Noel.

"Tell us about yourself, first," said the woman on the other end of the line.

"Like what?" said Noel. "If I like mustard on my pretzels? If I'm allergic to bees?"

"What we'd really like," the woman said, "would be your name and Social Security number."

"Name's Tollah," Noel said, in the conversation, which was recorded, and which we have had the opportunity to listen to. "Alan Tollah," he said, and he must have had the organizer opened to the page marked "Personal & Private."

"Social Security number?" the woman said.

"Could you give me an easier one first?" Noel asked. "Something less personal?"

"Place of birth?" said the woman.

"OK," said Noel, glancing at the Filofax, "I was born in Paterson, New Jersey, on a dark and stormy night."

The FBI was not amused. "How are you spelling Paterson," she asked, and then asked Noel to hold. "Sure," he said and broke the connection.

*   *   *

Three A.M. Can't sleep. Keep reaching around in bed for a female body . Finally, I got up, switched on the light and then the electric typewriter. I weigh 196 pounds. That's one good reason to be unhappy.

The reasons I have to be happy are:

1. I'm not disappointing anybody.
   a) Other than myself.
2. I'm not making anybody sad.
   a) Other than myself.
3. Right now I don't hate anybody.
   a) Other than myself.
   b) My fat self.

But oddly, despite the melancholia, I can't shake the suspicion that now for some reason this is the beginning of my life. It is as if I were preparing to be born again. I find that I can smell, touch, feel, with an unfamiliar intensity. With an intensity which I had forgotten possible.

Lying on my back in bed, I feel just as I did in the Cincinnati Work House. There's an exquisite awareness of being and of pain. The sensation is precisely that of having had a three-penny nail driven through the sternum. First I'm aware of the cars on the parkway, then the refrigerator, and finally, in my ears, I can just make out the churning of a pulse. The sound grows louder, closer, becomes a roar. Like the crashing of surf against a rockbound coast. "I shot a man in Reno, just to watch him die."

10:03 A.M. At work. Nothing about the bomb in the papers. This is odd. I personally saw a couple of fire trucks and two dozen cops.

The following evening Noel drove to the mall outside of Peekskill to buy a new bathroom scale. Driving north on the Saw Mill River Parkway, then heading east toward the river on Route 6, he would have passed a billboard that read: "You have survived 29 serious nuclear safety violations. Close Indian Point."

"If this diet is going to work," he told his sister, in a rare phone call, "I need to be able to see the results. I wake up often with sand in my eyes and waste minutes every morning hanging onto the shower door, squinting down at the needle." He told Kat that he had gone into The General Store, a vast emporium in the Jefferson Valley Mall. The display on The Executive Weight Master was larger and more clearly visible.

```
Fulton Basque Holloway
Holloway, Holloway & Stone
230 Benefit Street
Providence, Rhode Island 02903
```

Tony:

I'm on a diet. The pounds are going to melt away. You won't recognize me. I won't recognize me.
Point of order:
When you take an office memo and scrawl one line across the top in purple flair pen, this does not count as intimate correspondence. Especially when your secretary is the one who's put it in the envelope. Congratulations, though, on becoming a partner.
You say that in your profession "money is something of a compensation." A compensation for what?

Love,
No

P.S. Yes, my sister is still attractive. Her
husband's the one beginning to show signs of
wear. I gather you aren't interested in him.

P.P.S. If this apartment building goes co-op,
should I buy? I don't want to be put out into
the street. "The foxes have holes, and the birds
of the air have nests, but the Son of man hath
no where to lay his head."

10

CREATE A DOCUMENT

TUESDAY, MARCH 13, 1984. 193 pounds. I've stopped gaining weight. What did Mao say? The longest diet begins with a single pound.

Ran with Giff and bet him $100 that I won't get involved with anybody even remotely female for at least a year. "It's all I've cared about since age eleven. I've been the pet to one woman or another since my junior year of high school."

GIFF: "A sex slave?"

ME: "Exactly. Only without the sex. Mostly we shop, take long rides in the countryside. Inclement weather we hang pictures, move the furniture around."

That Wednesday he saw Cleo. Although she denies it, Hammersmith reports that the doctor was visibly upset.

Wednesday Eve. Fight with shrink.

"You know we can't make any progress if you don't tell me what's going on," she said.

ME: "But I confide. My life is an open book."

CLEO: "What about your past?"

ME: "My past is so boring."

CLEO: "Even to you?"

ME: "Especially to me. Everybody knows the story. We start out happy, in harmony, and then we fall away from grace. Wordsworth wrote it: 'Shades of the prison-house begin to close./ Upon the growing Boy.'"

CLEO: "I wish you wouldn't try to escape into poetry when we're discussing biography."

ME: "Poetry is biography."

CLEO: "I'm not going to argue that. On the other hand I do need to know that you're not hiding some big event. Something even I might have heard of?"

ME: "Christ, but you're suspicious."

CLEO: "Paid to be."

ME: "I thought you were paid to make me happy. Or thin."

CLEO: "I'm not going to fight that one again. Let's start at the beginning. Or at least as close as you can recall. When did you first get the impression that you were worthless?"

ME: "Very early. About age six."

CLEO (pulled out her desk drawer, took out a pencil, and began to write with it on a yellow legal pad): "Anything happen that year? Anything in particular?"

ME: "I suppose then I was happy. I remember walking down the slate path from the driveway to the kitchen door and thinking, 'Soon I'll be six. The world is my oyster.' And I'd never eaten an oyster."

CLEO: "So with such a promising start, what happened?"

ME: "The girl was born. My sister was born."

CLEO: "And?"

ME: "Kat was sickly. I know now they didn't expect her to live. They kept her in bed with them."

CLEO: "What was the matter with your sister?"

ME: "She was dramatically underweight and prey to a series of infections. Finally antibiotics cleared them up. But it was touch and go."

CLEO: "Were you aware of the seriousness of the situation?"

ME: "Probably not. They kept her in bed, though. I knew that."

CLEO: "Who kept her in bed?"

ME: "My mother and father. They kept her in bed with them."

CLEO: "In bed. Are you certain?"

ME: "Of course not. I was six years old. I do have this image though, and maybe it's invented, of me walking in on her in bed with my mother, having a big feed."

CLEO: "Eating?"

ME: "Being breast-fed."

CLEO: "And how did that make you feel?"

ME: "I guess I must have been disgusted."

```
Fulton Basque Holloway
Holloway, Holloway & Stone
230 Benefit Street
Providence, Rhode Island 02903

Tony:

He lives. He writes. I'd given up hope.
Certainly we can have dinner Monday. How about
the Oyster Bar? No, I still don't make what you
so delicately call "real money." The entire
publishing industry seems to have taken a strict
vow of poverty.


Love
No,
```

Thursday, March 15, 1984. Happy Birthday to me. Shelley was dead at 30, Christ at 33. I'm 35 and haven't done a thing. Unless there's something I don't remember. Has there ever been a great man who had no recollection of his deeds? A sort of reverse Jekyll and Hyde?

I am losing weight. Oh, how I want to be thin. Really thin. I mean skeletal. So far I'm down to 190 lbs.

Ran with Giff and his black buddy again. The Pig showed up at the last minute. He was wearing a gray, charcoal-striped suit and red suspenders, looking chubby and wistful. Fortunately, we were already changed and so managed to avoid inviting him.

We went eight miles, up to the wire factory and back.

Giff mentioned that I'm an editor.

The black guy was impressed: "Where?"

ME: "Acropolis."

BLACK GUY: "The best little publishing house in America."

ME: "That's right. Although actually we're not. There are smaller houses. And better ones as well."

BLACK GUY: "What's your specialty?"

ME: "Books."

BLACK GUY: "And what sort of books."

ME (mumbling): "Diet books."

BLACK GUY: "What?"

ME: "Diet books."

BLACK GUY: "You write diet books?"

ME: "Edit them. Mostly I edit them."

End of conversation. End of all conversations. It was almost enough to make me wish we'd waited for the Pig.

In Lincoln's time, there was a law in North Carolina against teaching blacks to read. A white man who gave or sold a book to a slave could be fined $200. This was true for any book, even the Bible. Feature a book being that important today. Would you fine somebody for selling or even giving out copies of *The Grape-fruit Diet*?

Tuesday, March 20, 1984. I weigh 187 pounds. That's progress. Tony came all right. We never made it to the dining room. We stayed in the Oyster Bar saloon and drank our supper. Tony favors Scotch. I like gin. Beefeater. "The imported one."

The next morning I found ketchup on my necktie. Ketchup or Tabasco sauce. Did we have oysters?

Meeting with Tony is a little like going down in a diving bell. We find a comfortable place to sit, fasten our seat belts, and then drink to a depth of extreme amiability. Sometimes I can actually hear my ears popping. He wanted to know about my sister. I told him again that she is married. Happily married. Which is a lie, but then I'm tired of my role as family pimp.

My friends have always been interested in my sister. Many guys were friends with me because of my sister. This had not been true of Tony. Why? He had the wrong sort of looks for my sister. (Bad ones.) Wrong sort of personality. (Bad also.) Now that he's rich, I suppose that's all changed.

Tony and I were roommates in Boston when I first got out of college. Tony was working at the Cambridge Public Library and writing a novel. I was working as an attendant in a mental hospital and writing a play. We read George Orwell together, Aldous Huxley, Herman Hesse (blush), took mescaline. Which killed more brain cells, I wonder, the *Siddartha* or the mescaline?

Then I fell in love with Polly Blaine. Then he fell in love with Polly Blaine. Then he married Polly Blaine. Then he reconciled with his rich father, went to law school, went to work for the firm. He went from being a feckless youth to being a young man of promise in the course of about three fucks. Polly is the sort of girl who used to be known as a good influence.

I had a bad patch. I had been smoking a good deal of dope at the time as well, which didn't exactly give me a clear head with which to face my suddenly empty world. Polly threw me over for Tony. Tony threw me over for Polly. "A friend dead is to be mourned. A friend married is to be guarded against, both being equally lost." That's from the diary of C. S. Lewis. Then my parents were killed. I began to have these memory lapses.

Tony and I don't see each other that much anymore, but the deal is still that in a crisis we will each be home to the other one. The final refuge. The line is from Frost's *Death of the Hired Man*. "Home is where you find it." No, that's not Frost, that's the Smirnoff ad. Frost: "Home is the place where, when you have to go there, they have to take you in." Frost's got another definition of home. Here we go: "Something you somehow haven't to deserve." Which would also make a splendid ad for vodka.

We had a lot in common. There's not much left. Outside of the fact that I had loved the woman he bedded nightly. That's sweet Polly, the one he's now intent on leaving. And there's one other shared quality: We both think we're too good for this world. Tony's a lawyer. Tony doesn't want to be a lawyer. He wants to be a novelist. I'm an editor. I don't want to be an editor. I want to be a playwright. So we get together, the playwright and the novelist, and we drink. Until finally one of us gets sick. Usually it's me, lawyers having iron stomachs.

This time we made a plan. Actually Tony made the plan. Secretly, he's even more ambitious for literary fame than am I. We will write letters, many letters. Sharpen our skills. Leave tracks. Create a document.

11

MEANINGFUL CHANGE

After a session in early April, Dr. Santarelli reports that her patient began to act out. He stopped near the door and tried to kiss his psychiatrist. "He's not your standard rapist," she told us. "More pathetic, really, than threatening." The doctor pushed her impertinent charge away. "This sort of thing is fatal to the process," she told him.

"I'm sorry," Noel said. "Did I spoil your lipstick?"

"No," said Cleo. "But you will spoil the therapy."

"Maybe with your love I won't need therapy," Noel said.

"Let's fix your life first," Cleo said.

"If I were thinner?" Noel asked. "And didn't have spots on my face. Would you love me then?"

"I like you now," said Cleo.

"I don't want to be liked," said Noel. "Not by you. Not by any woman."

"For the moment," said Cleo, "let's take the calorie count and the love factor out of the equation. Don't you have other issues? Don't you have any other ambitions?"

"I don't believe in God," said Noel. "I'm not even sure I believe in individual action. I'm sure I don't believe in the system. Which leaves what?"

"You tell me," said Cleo, who remembers that she had sat back down, even though the session was officially over. She began taking notes. "Nobody knocked," she told us, "so my next appointment must have canceled. I asked him, 'You must believe in something.' "

"What should I believe in? Art? The Almighty Dollar?"

"Something."

"Women," said Noel. "I believe in women."

"Now you *are* exaggerating," said Cleo.

"I don't think so," said Noel. "I'm only being sincere. I like the way the women smell. I like to touch them, hear them talk to one another. There's no more glorious music than the sound of two women talking at a distance, where you can't make out the words, and especially if one of those women is your lover. I even enjoy hearing them breathe."

"What about values?"

"That's the beauty of it. Each woman comes with her own complete set of values. It's better not to have your own. They'll just get in the way."

"Now you're trying to be comic," said Cleo.

"No, I'm not. Look at my history. First I was in love with a girl named Mousie, although she didn't know that I was in love with her. We never even kissed. I did start running, though. Which was her sport. Then there was Polly. Polly was the first woman I screwed. She was so impressed with my performance in bed that she married my best friend. I took my first editing job to support Louise as a writer. Louise was in love with Hemingway. She had read all his books. Had pictures of him under the glass of her office desk. So I read all his books, too. She was very passionate at first. Even shaved her head, so we could reenact that scene from *For Whom the Bell Tolls.* The earth moved. Trouble was, we modeled our relationship on the works of Hemingway. So one of us was supposed to die young. Whenever I went out for a drive, or climbed a stepladder, Louise would grow agitated. I think now that she expected me to die. Which I didn't do. Finally, she lost patience and we split up.

"Moved from White Plains to the building I now inhabit, because Helen was in a studio apartment there and thought she'd like a one-bedroom and couldn't afford it without me. Helen was in love with Paul Newman. We watched his movies. We drank his lemonade. Ultimately, of course, she got somebody who looked more like Newman than I did. I don't actually look that much like Paul Newman. Do I?" he asked, and presented Cleo with his profile. "I mean if Paul Newman were chubby? And had acne scars?'"

"No," she said. "You don't look much like Paul Newman. Even if he were chubby."

"Well," said Noel. "When I lost the Paul Newman look-alike contest, I lost Helen. Sally liked the apartment and didn't mind where I worked as long as she had time in the middle of the day to fuck somebody else. Sally was in love with Dylan. Listened to his music endlessly. God how I grew to hate that voice. She left me, too, quite suddenly. Of course she wrote a terrible song about it. Then I met Martha. Book editor was an appropriate position for me to be in while Martha finished up her graduate schooling at Columbia. Martha was a passionate advocate of birth control, actually tithed to Planned Parenthood. I did too while we were together. She was in love with Philip Roth. I don't look much like Philip Roth, do I?"

"No," said, Cleo, "you don't."

"I mean if Philip Roth were chubby."

"Not even if Philip Roth were very fat," said Cleo.

"Right," said Noel. "I stayed on at the job so that Ginny could paint. "

"Who was Ginny in love with?"

"Lots of people."

"So everything you've done up until now has been in response to the imagined needs of women?"

"Imagined or not imagined," Noel told his psychiatrist. "I still think birth control is a good idea."

```
Fulton Basque Holloway
Holloway, Holloway & Stone
230 Benefit Street
Providence, Rhode Island 02903


Tony:


     Now this letter you're going to answer,
right? Remember the deal? Famous after death.
They won't produce my plays. Nor will they
publish your novels. But you and I, we have a
```

clever plan. What are we going to do? We're
going to die. (Which probably will happen
anyway.)

. Then somebody stumbles on our letters. Which
are irresistible. Who knew how tender and tragic
those two men were? First the document is handed
around. Then published. Suddenly, we're recognized. Just like Heloise and Abelard. Well, not
just like Heloise and Abelard, but close enough
for today's discerning public.

Writing letters may seem a little ridiculous
but honestly, Tony, it's our only chance. One
simply can't phone his way into Benet's Reader's
Encyclopedia.

If you're smart, you'll keep a journal as
well. This way they can read you unburdening
yourself to me, and also you unburdening yourself to the person you love the most in the
world: yourself.

The very fact that we've amounted to nothing,
it'll work to our advantage. Look at Emily Dickinson. Because she wouldn't stop for death, he
kindly stopped for her. Nobody else ever did.
Alive she couldn't get arrested. Dead she's the
Belle of Amherst.

Apparently, it's better if the life illuminated has been difficult and without
distinction. I don't know about difficult, but
you and I, we sure got ignominious in a corner.

Love,
No

Wednesday, April 18, 1984. 2:11 P.M. 183 lbs. If you jiggle the Weight Master.

Che's going to have to delay his book for at least a year. Called me up. He said his father's got a big job. "A contract with a utility company."

ME: "Where?"

CHE: "Near Peekskill."

ME: "Where near Peekskill?"

CHE: "Indian Point."

ME: "Where the bomb is?"

CHE: "You mean the nuclear reactor?"

ME: "I mean the bomb."

CHE: "Yes, we're working in the plant that has the nuclear reactor. One of them."

I pray God he's better with structure structure than he is with sentence structure.

Kat phoned yesterday. She never calls.

She said she wants to leave Doctor Bill.

ME: "Why?"

LITTLE SISTER: "I think I want to wait until I'm older before I marry a doctor. I mean I don't really need him. I'm in perfect health. Even Bill says I'm as strong as a horse. Plus I'm bored. Doctors are so boring when you're not sick."

ME: "You bore easily. You used to like him."

LITTLE SISTER: "He used to send me flowers."

ME: "He doesn't send you flowers anymore?"

LITTLE SISTER: "Not unless I ask."

ME: "Flowers are no good if they're asked for?"

LITTLE SISTER: "Of course not. I feel so pent up, so controlled. It's a sort of poverty. When I was single my pockets did jingle."

ME: "Did not."

LITTLE SISTER: "Come on. It'll be fun. We could double-date."

ME: "I don't want to date. I'm too old to double-date."

LITTLE SISTER: "What do you mean too old? You're still a baby."

ME: "I was born too old to double-date. Please don't leave Bill."

LITTLE SISTER: "It's either leave him, or murder him in his bath."

ME: "So tell me. On a totally different subject. Or almost totally different. How *do* you get a woman to love you?"

LITTLE SISTER: "That's easy. You bring her flowers."

Some time in April, 1984. 6:33 P.M. I brought Cleo flowers, which she accepted with a smile. With a weary smile. Then I told her about the success of my diet. I showed her how loose my pants are. She was not pleased. That's where we differ. Cleo doesn't see that weight loss constitutes meaningful change.

12

FOR WHOMSOEVER BEATH ON NATIONAL TELEVISION

CAME INTO THE locker room at the Business Man's Club and found the black guy; his name is Tom Janus. He was in a huddle with Giff. I walked up behind them, and they were startled, sprang apart as if they'd been surprised in a crime.

ME: "What were you talking about?"

GIFF: "Nothing."

ME: "Didn't look like nothing."

GIFF: "You really want to know?"

ME: "Yup."

GIFF: "You. We were talking about you. What could be more fascinating?"

Which has to be a lie. Then we all went for a run. Giff, the black guy, and the Pig. Giff and the Pig spoke briefly, about baseball, what chance the Mets had. Giff's a Yankee fan. I guess you figured that one out.

Then the Pig made speeches. It might have been Tom that set the Oinker off. Something about being in the presence of a genuine minority member that gives us Caucasians a moral hard-on. You don't want *them* to suppose that *you* think social injustice tolerable. First the Pig told us about his involvement in the antiwar movement (minimal). Then he mentioned the story he'd seen on the evening news about a guy who was claiming to have been the real David Berkowitz.

PIG: "What galls me is that anybody would want to be David Berkowitz. The Son of Sam went out in the evenings with a revolver hidden in a plastic garbage bag and killed young people who were necking."

ME: "He wasn't even a very good shot."

GIFF: "We all know who he is."

PIG: "That's why he did it. Or, if not, it's why the next guy will."

GIFF: "How do you know what David Berkowitz thinks?"

PIG: "Same way I know what you think."

GIFF: "You run with David Berkowitz?"

PIG: "No, I don't run with David Berkowitz. He's a human being. So am I."

GIFF (grinning widely): "Oooh weee. I don't know who to congratulate here."

Fulton Basque Holloway
Holloway, Holloway & Stone
230 Benefit Street
Providence, Rhode Island 02903

Tony:

  Yes, little sister did call about you. No, I didn't tell her that you've been made a full partner. The woman doesn't need encouragement. You'd be husband number four.

  I strongly suggest though that you see a shrink before you start up with Katherine Moses Hammersmith. Might turn out there's another more

sensible option. Like shooting yourself in the
roof of the mouth.

I'm seeing a shrink myself. She's a woman.
She thinks my problem is that I'm afraid of
women. I think my problem is that I'm poor, fat,
short, and disappointed. Also I'm afraid of
women.

Love,
No

Tuesday, May 8, 1984. It's 6 P.M. I weigh 181 pounds. Campbell
came by this afternoon all excited. Archer's been fired. Now our
entire editorial policy is going to be set by a helicopter pilot.

Son of Sam came up again today during the run. Same crew,
similar discussion.

PIG: "I saw Berkowitz mentioned in a piece about journal-
keeping, how and why."

ME: "I keep a journal."

GIFF: "Must be riveting."

ME: "Thanks."

GIFF: "I mean your life is *so* thrilling. You keep asking the
eternal question: Did I eat a bagel? Did I eat two bagels? Plus,
there's nothing like celibacy to move a plot along."

ME: "Fuck you!"

PIG: "Look, I'm trying to have a discussion here."

GIFF: "Discuss away."

PIG: "They had a box with the important people who had
kept journals: Samuel Pepys, Leo Tolstoy, Henry David
Thoreau, and David Berkowitz. He's famous. He's a famous
writer."

GIFF: "So maybe that's what this other guy thought. Maybe
that's why he wanted to claim to be the Son of Sam. Get his
poetry published. But who cares? It's still bad poetry."

ME: "I care."

We ran hard for a couple of hundred yards to try and lose the Pig, but he kept right up. As soon as we slowed, he started in again. "When I watch the evening news, I feel like I'm drinking battery acid, and it's going right to my values."

GIFF: "You have values?"

PIG: "Yeah, I have values."

GIFF: "Congratulations then."

PIG: "On what?"

GIFF: "On keeping them under wraps the way you do."

PIG: "Fuck you. All I ever did was make a lot of money. I still have values. And when compared to those expressed by the evening news, I'm practically a North Pole Saint. I believe, for instance, that it's possible to be a worthwhile person without being either rich or notorious."

GIFF: "This may come as a shock to you, but the people I know who work in television agree. None of us think that you have to be rich and famous in order to be worthwhile."

PIG: "I don't know what the people who work in TV would argue, but I am familiar with the message they broadcast, and that message is that it's a big deal to be on TV, the biggest deal. It's a blessing. And who do they bless? The bad guys."

ME (watching Tom to make sure this didn't offend him): "He's right. They have inflated racism out of all proportion, not as a stab at justice, but as a new form of entertainment. They celebrate murderers, rapists, and politicians who are either grandstanding or corrupt. When it comes to ordinary people, they bless ordinary people only to the extent that they have exhibited exceptional wickedness, or at least been touched by it. When black men kill Jews, or Jews kill black men, that's when they get on TV."

GIFF: "There are reasons the news people do what they do. It's a competitive business. We are expected to turn a profit. Else we lose our jobs."

PIG: "Sure, I know. Conflict makes the best story. So the news is splitting us apart."

GIFF: "There was conflict before the television. Also violence."

PIG: "Yeah, but the violence was beside the point. Now it is the point."

Giff scowled back at the Pig. "You been eating righteous cereal?" he asked. "Who put the bug up your ass?"

ME: "Listen, I agree with the Pig here, I mean Peas," I said, but he didn't seem to have noticed the insult. "Legitimate conflict, fine. You want to re-create the Lincoln/Douglas debates, I'm with you. This is not what we have on TV, though. What we have on TV is show biz."

GIFF (looking my way): "I can't believe you're siding with this guy. Don't tell me you're also in favor of the flat tax?"

PIG: "You may not like it Giff, but the No Man is right. Public discourse has been reduced to entertainment. Nobody's in control."

GIFF: "Why is this any worse than it's always been?"

PIG: "For a whole host of reasons. There used to be lots of potent counteractive forces: the church, Temple, the family, the hometown. Show biz was not respectable in the old days, nor was it so powerful. And the technology is better than it has ever been, better than Orwell could have imagined."

GIFF: "I suppose."

ME: "They don't want to bring us together through serious debate, they want to keep us glued to the convertible sofa. So they harp on racism, and the war between the sexes. Tragic accidents. Blizzards. Anything that'll hold interest."

GIFF: "Books, I suppose, are wonderful."

ME: "Books are not as bad."

GIFF: "Why's that?"

ME: "With books you actually have to move your eyes. Besides which, books aren't all the same. Or not yet. On TV, everything has an identical subtext."

IG: "That's right. Listen to him."

GIFF: "Remember, it's my rice bowl you're cracking."

ME: "Watch the news and you come away with the distinct impression that nothing really has substance anymore outside of money, power, and notoriety. Money beats virtue every time, power beats money, and notoriety tops them all."

GIFF: "When did you get to be such a prig?"

ME (pretending not to have heard the last jibe): "So a person can spend his entire life teaching poor children how to read, and after all is said and done, nobody gives a shit. He's a sap. If one of his little students is elected president of the United States—not bloody likely—our hero will get three minutes on Charles Kuralt. Alternatively, he can purchase a handgun, rape, and shoot three nuns. Suddenly he's the subject of national curiosity. A curiosity which borders on adoration."

TOM (speaking up for one of the first times ever): "Would you do something to stop this?"

ME: "What?"

TOM: "I don't know. But if you could do something, would you?"

ME: "Sure, I suppose."

TOM (nodding): "Good."

PIG: "In the meantime, we're all being encouraged to shoot nuns."

GIFF: "If you shoot nuns, they will also put you in jail."

PIG: "A nice jail. With a law library and a color TV."

GIFF: "Jails aren't really all that nice. The chow, for instance, is disgusting."

ME: "Maybe so, but then you've got the attention of the world. You've become a real, an actual person. Hated perhaps, but also cared for. Cared about. That's worth any amount of cafeteria food. You're immortal. Holy, Holy, Holy. You'll never die. For whomsoever beath on national TV, that man shall never die."

13

GOOD BUSINESS

Editor's Note: The journal entries become so irregular at this point that it's hard to know precisely when and where we are. The more weight he lost, the more money he earned, the less Noel wrote. Finally he got so thin, he stopped writing altogether. And yet what happened—the purchase of the public relations book, the meeting with his next woman—is simply too important to be left out.]

After he'd lost fifteen pounds, Noel stopped seeing the psychiatrist. He'd run out his program and would have had to pay for any additional visits, but also they actually had a fight. Dr. Santarelli learned that both Noel's parents had been killed in a bombing incident in Israel. The following dialogue is taken from notes that Dr. Santarelli has been kind enough to share.

"How could you hide this? The trauma might have led directly to your memory lapses," she said.

"You're wrong," said Noel. "I'm very very sorry that my parents died. But I don't actually think it's all that significant."

"What is important then?" Dr. Santarelli asked.

"I need to find a girlfriend, get down to my ideal weight."

"If you were to get right to the core of your despair," Cleo asked, "what would you say it was about?"

"It's about weighing too much. It's also about powerlessness. It's catching a glimpse of this pitiful monster in the mirror. Having that red ring around my waist when I undress at night."

"Panty hose makes that sort of ring, no matter how thin you are," Cleo said.

"I know that," said Noel. "And knowing it doesn't help. Men are never Rubenesque, doctor. I'm in a trap, with one way out: thinness. You know what fatness says? It says I'm self-indulgent, it says I'm weak. It says I'm sexually ambiguous. Make me thin, or make me famous."

"Well, in that case," the doctor said, and she remembers putting away her notepad as she spoke, "I can't rightly take your money."

"I've stopped seeing a psychiatrist," Noel told Kat in a phone call shortly after this exchange. "Now I won't need to be so God damned cheerful."

By late spring 1985, our hero had dropped to 150 pounds. He'd been on Stillman's all-protein diet, on Dr. Atkins Diet Revolution. Finally he was eating one butterscotch sundae every twenty-four hours. He had memory lapses but didn't mind nearly as much because when he woke up, he was thinner. The journal kicked back into life in the summer of 1985, at about the time of his final promotion.

Tuesday, August 13, 1985. 2:11 P.M. I'm still on the 37th floor of the Pan Am Building. In a different office. Alan Tollah's old office. Tah! Dah! This is definitely the office. You can tell because it's way too big. Big enough for badminton. Also, it's in the corner.

Turns out the Ayatollah likes me. He's made me editor in chief. "I don't know anything about books," he told me with a little more satisfaction than seemed absolutely necessary in a book publisher. "We need you," he said, after calling me into his office and closing the door. "We need your talent. And your scruples."

This is a clear case of what my little sister calls The Law of Contrary. "The adult human rarely tells the truth, but some humans will sometimes present you with its exact opposite."

Examples: The butcher says that while there are tradesmen who will short-weight their customers, this butcher, the one talking, will not. "I should lie to good people like you, in order to make a couple of extra bucks?" he asks a perfect stranger. "Life's too short." What he's actually telling you is that he's short-weighting your boned leg of lamb. Look closely, and you'll see his thumb on the scale. He knows that because he's raised the issue of morality, you're much less likely to question his own. Same with the cabby who says some cabbies will take you all over town. That cabby will take you all over town.

So clearly the Ayatollah thinks I'm stupid and morally bankrupt.

Alan Tollah himself has moved to still larger digs on the 36th floor. Even when he was up here, though, he was a big noise in marketing. I guess this means I'm a big noise in editorial, although I don't feel very loud yet. When I go out into the hallway, nobody exactly falls on his face. Or her face. Campbell seems not to have noticed at all. He was at my desk when I came back from lunch. On the phone. Cordovan Weejuns on the blotter. Sounded like he was arranging to have somebody look at his gums. Probably a dentist. Although with Frank you never know for sure.

I waited politely at Amelia's station. Amelia is the editorial secretary and so has been moved into the tiny room that adjoins the badminton court. The one Pip Pip used to have. Amelia was still out, or powdering her nose. Finally, Frank got off the phone, muttered something about privacy, there not being any.

"Thanks, No," he said, distractedly, as he shuffled by. Meaning thanks Noel, I hope. Although he could have meant, no thanks. This is possible. He must be a little ticked off about my being in here. He was a senior staff editor when I was still a pup.

Wednesday, August 14, 1985, 4 P.M. Amelia helped me clean out my former desk and filing cabinet. I found three pairs of tube socks. Also nineteen virgin manuscripts. When I say virgin, I mean they still had their rubber bands on. Looking closely at the cover letters was enough to convince me that five of them could be turned down on the spot. A sixth has already been published by Norton and is right now number eight on the *Publishers Weekly* best-seller list. The other manuscripts, the undecideds, went onto my new sofa.

[Editor's Note: The details of the following transaction are not made entirely clear in Noel's journal. What is not in dispute is that Campbell went into the badminton court one afternoon with a manuscript that he dropped immediately into the trash, and then did his famous imitation of a toilet flushing.]

"What's that?" Noel asked.

"Vile," said Campbell.

"Should I look at it?"

"No," Campbell said, and left. And so Noel fished the pages out of the wastepaper basket. The manuscript was titled *Finding a Cure: The True Story of the Lily White Chemical Corporation*. The letter attached suggested that the writers—employees at a public relations firm known as PBCD and O—expected Acropolis to pay $25,000 for the right to publish a 357-page advertising supplement. Noel dropped the manuscript back into the wastebasket.

The following morning, he was contacted by a man named George Soper. "I'm calling for Wilson Peters," said Soper. "Can you put me in touch with Noel Hammersmith?"

Thursday, August 15, 1985. A compliment. A palpable compliment. From a citizen of the great female nation. A woman named Peters, Wilson Peters. "Let me make sure I've got this right," she said. "Are you the genius behind the all-poison diet?"

I allowed as how I was the genius behind the all-poison diet. "Do you want me to refer you to our legal department?" I asked.

"No, no," said the woman. "I love the idea. A witty diet. Why hasn't anybody thought up something like that before?"

I asked again if she wanted to be referred to the legal department.

"No," said the woman. "You misconstrue. I'm a fan."

I tried not to sound relieved. The diet had been commercially successful, but it had also attracted a firestorm of negative publicity. Nobody had died, but several children had become seriously ill after eating the treated food of their fat parents.

"We need to talk," said the woman. "You aren't free for dinner tonight, are you?"

I admitted that I was free for dinner.

Then she asked me to hang on for a moment, and I could hear her speaking tartly to somebody in the background. Something about the airlines, and her not having promised anything until the beginning of next week. Then she pitched her voice back at me.

"Sorry, sorry," she said. "Busy, busy. Can I take you to dinner?"

I said OK, but felt oddly unmanned by the suggestion. Aren't we supposed to take them to dinner?

"So why don't you come up here, then. At around 6:30 P.M. We're not far. The PBCD and O building on Madison. Twelfth floor. That all right?" she asked, but then hung up before I had time to respond.

Friday, August 16. By 5:55 I was in the foyer on the twelfth floor of the PBCD and O building on Madison Avenue. I gave my name. I sat in one of two armchairs, leafed through an old copy of *Vanity Fair*. There was a picture of Jeff Bridges on the cover.

A young woman appeared. She was a little bit fat. That was the first thing I noticed. Judge not and ye shall not be judged. She was a good ten pounds overweight. Otherwise she was gorgeous. Late twenties and with auburn hair, to the waist. She introduced herself as Wilson Peters.

Then I stood up. Then I put my foot in it.

ME: "But you're not the vice president?"

FAT WOMAN: "Last time I checked."

She chose the restaurant. She didn't want wine.

I asked why.

"Well," she said, and blushed, "I'm eating for two now." Then she gave me that one-of-a-kind grin they all have and reserve for precisely this occasion. I think they must learn it from watching old movies. We, the men, are supposed to be delighted. It's as if underpopulation were a pressing international problem.

ME: "No husband, boyfriend?"

WILSON: "Tant mieux."

I don't know what that means, but I don't think it could be good. You made your bed, fella, now lie in it. That's what I thought. Not what I said. White man speaks with forked tongue. What I said was, "If there's ever anything I can do to help."

Afterward, she was going back to the office. I walked her there. We paused in the lobby. Was I supposed to kiss the vice president? I didn't think so. She said I look a little bit like Jeff Bridges.

"Really," I said. "I never heard that one before." Afterward, I sort of fade out. I must have gone to Grand Central. I must have taken the last train home. I'm here in the office again today. With a fresh shirt. Reading the paper. There's a story about a bomb that went off last night somewhere in the Village. This blew up a trash can. Two dogs were killed. A professional dog walker is now in intensive care.

All through dinner I was having two thoughts:

1. Gosh but she's pretty.

2. What's this really about?

We never spoke of my diet books. We never touched on business of any sort.

Friday, August 16, 1985. Evening. She said she'd call me the next day. That was today. She didn't call. Finally, I called her. Got the secretary. His name is George.

GEORGE: "Who shall I say is calling?

ME: "Noel Hammersmith."

GEORGE (a minute later): "I'm afraid Ms. Peters is busy now. What can I tell her this is in reference to?"

ME: "Nothing."

The following conversation has been reconstructed after extensive interviews with Francis Gifford Bates (aka Giff).

"It was like 8 A.M. on Sunday. I was still in bed," Noel told Giff when they ran together on the following Monday.

"Alone?" Giff asked.

"Alone," said Noel, and waited for Giff to pry. Giff did not pry. The two men ran in silence for a couple of minutes.

"Without coffee I'm legally dead," Noel said. "I hadn't had my coffee."

"Why?"

"She said it was an emergency."

"Doesn't she live in the city?"

"It turns out she lives in Connecticut, about half an hour from my apartment. She said her garage door was jammed. The cat was trapped inside. Without food or water. She said I'd said if there was anything I could ever do to help."

"And?" said Giff.

"I got there. The house is right on the road. I rang the doorbell. Knocked. No sound. Not even a car on the road behind me. Thought I must have the wrong address. Then I had that feeling you get when somebody off camera is watching you."

"And there she was," Giff said. "In Saran Wrap?"

"No, not exactly. But stunning. Before this, I'd only seen Wilson in a suit, you know. With shoulder pads. Now she was wearing jeans, torn at one knee, a blue T-shirt with "Carpe diem" written across the belly in white script. She looked about 16. Sixteen and slightly pregnant. She was wearing a battered man's fedora. Oh, and there was something else.

A broom. She was holding a broom." The two man ran in silence for a mile or so.

"OK," said Giff. "You've got my interest. What happened?"

"It started raining," said Noel. "I was invited inside. The house smelled of gingerbread. She gave me a hand towel to dry my hair with. Then she asked if I wanted coffee."

"And you said yes," said Giff.

"I asked her if it was made. It was not made. I asked her if she was making any for herself. She patted her belly. 'We can't,' she said."

Giff wagged his head sadly, "And I bet you didn't get any coffee either. That sort of pussy."

"I wasn't thinking coffee right then," said Noel. "She gave me a tour."

"Yeah," said Giff.

"It's exactly the sort of house that real estate ads describe as 'loaded with charm.' "

"I know," said Giff. "Bad plumbing and insect damage."

"I don't know about the insects," said Noel. "The building was originally a toll house. You need to stoop in order to move from room to room. I followed her little butt around. First it got so I couldn't talk. Then it got so that I couldn't breathe. In the living room she had art photographs. 'My brilliant cousin,' she explained. 'He's actually an optometrist.' You've seen pictures like this: A falling-down barn, a park bench with nobody sitting on it. Black and white. Eight by ten. Exactly like Walker Evans, only nothing like Walker Evans."

"Art's an aphrodisiac," said Giff. "Even bad art. Especially bad art. So you made your move? Please, please tell me you made your move."

"I put my arms around her waist," said Noel, and even now, a day later, his voice thickened. "She took my hand, led me upstairs and into a bedroom. 'I have to go to the bathroom,' she said. 'You take off your clothes.' "

"And you did?"

"I did."

"Good boy," said Giff. "Then what?"

"Then nothing," said Noel.

"I always tell you."

"You're different than I am."

"OK, OK!" Giff said, and left it at that. But he was sore.

Noel did write up the scene that night in his journal. He thought he might use it in a play.

I sat on a chair, with my legs crossed, and my hands where the fig leaf is traditionally placed. Wilson came out of the bathroom without her pants on, and got into bed. "Don't you want to lie down?" She asked.

I said I did.

WILSON: "Why don't you get into bed?"

So I did. And there was trouble. This probably had something to do with her being a vice president, and so willing.

We took a break. There followed fifteen minutes of extremely awkward conversation. "Do you enjoy tennis?" That sort of chat, with this woman sitting cross-legged on the bed, fiddling with the end of her braid, those pretty brows in a knot. "All dressed up, and no place to go." That's what she said. She was wearing the T-shirt and a pair of panties.

We started to neck. I fulfilled my manly responsibilities, although not with any sort of aplomb. By this time I had a dreadful lack-of-coffee headache. She offered me a glass of red wine. This was exactly what I did not need. I accepted.

"You might as well drink up," she said, when we'd settled in the living room and I took my first, tentative sip. "Stafford loved the stuff. The garage is full of it. I'm not supposed to touch alcohol until I go into false labor."

John Stafford seemed to have been the father. They broke up. "We were over," she said. I listened carefully, but there seemed to be no bitterness in this announcement. "Tant mieux," she said again.

She didn't get animated until she spoke of her former boyfriend's professional life. Stafford had worked for Ogilvy and Mather. She told me that she had once met David Ogilvy and considered him a great man. "So courtly."

ME: "That's what I've heard."

WILSON: "Advertising is our highest art form."

I nodded, but didn't lie.

WILSON: "You don't believe me?"

ME: "I don't know. I hadn't really thought about it."

WILSON: "No, really. It makes sense. When we had a religious society, people were hired to glorify God. Or they volunteered, but most often they were hired. Michelangelo, for instance. He was hired."

ME: "Now it's ScotTowels that we're hired to glorify."

WILSON (still serious): "Well, yes, and Volvo, and Apple computers. The very best young minds in the world work on those accounts."

ME: "And nobody can deny that ScotTowels exist."

In other, and totally unrelated news, my sister left her husband. How do I know? Dr. Bill called me last night. I could hear that he was smoking, and also the tinkle of ice in a tumbler. His voice was hoarse. Either the doctor had a bad cold, or else he'd been crying.

Wilson Peters came to Noel's actual workstation two days later and delivered a second copy of *Finding a Cure*.

[Editor's note: According to Noel's journal, it was with genuine reluctance that he raised the subject at the next meeting of the editorial board.] Campbell is reported to have had a violent allergy attack when the manuscript was mentioned. The recording secretary was dispatched to get him some paper towels. Eventually he stopped sneezing. "This is no country for old men," he muttered, but when Tollah asked him to speak up, he said, "Nothing, nothing," and only blew his nose.

"The book is written," Noel told Tollah. "It's quite readable. Although it's also an advertisement. They had originally wanted $25,000. I'm sure they'll settle for $5,000. PBCD and O will handle the publicity for free. All we have to do is stamp the manuscript print and distribute the books."

"Might it sell?" the Ayatollah asked.

Noel said it might.

The Ayatollah nodded. "I don't know anything about books," he said. "But I do know something about business. This sounds like good business."

14

PUSSY LITE

THURSDAY, OR IS IT Wednesday? I'm trying to escape the prison of self. So in this and future journals I will refer to myself as "Noel" instead of "Me." This gives me perspective. As if I were somebody else. In the meantime, I'm concentrating on others. People who are actually somebody else. Like Brad. Brad's an older guy. He's even slower than I am. Sometimes we'll all run together. He's fun to listen to. Bushy eyebrows. Very much the corporate counsel.

"First we'll sell them separately," Brad said, once we'd hit the relative quiet of the sidewalk on Sutton Place, "like radar detection units. Then I plan to go to GM. Or Volvo."

Giff wanted to know how the device would work.

"We've already got the technology," Brad said. "Go under the dashboard and install a hair dryer with Naugahyde or soft rubber lips. The costliest units, the Regal or Golden Geisha, would have surgical rubber. Maybe even silk. The Yeoman would cost half as much and be lined with canvas or burlap."

GIFF: "Ouch!"

BRAD: "The blowmaster opens out like an ashtray. Insert roger."

NOEL: "Isn't there some danger of a short circuit?"

BRAD: "In true love, sure, but not with my machine. They know how to ground out electrical engines that work in water."

GIFF: "That's right. I love my wet vac. I think you'd better start with Volvo, the Scandinavians are more open-minded. It would still take a real patriot to stick his dick into something made in Detroit."

NOEL: "And you need a better name."

BRAD: "I've got that. We'll call it the Cruise Hostess."

NOEL (nodding): "You have to use a doctor in the promotional drive. Can you make the device double as a brakeman's friend, something a man can piss into, if he's caught in traffic? Include a disposable plastic bag?"

BRAD: "Simple."

NOEL: "Good. Then get some M.D. to say how it's bad for men to delay micturition. Tie this in with prostate or bladder cancer. You could have a urologist on the poster, just the way they use cops in advertisements for antitheft equipment. Your model would wear a white jacket, and a stethoscope around his neck. 'I wish all of my patients had used the patented Cruise Hostess. Install this perfectly safe device today. Save wear and tear on your delicate urinary system. Never suffer from Rest Area panic again.' Play something from Charles Ives in the background."

BRAD: "I like it, Fatback. I can see why they value you so highly in the diet book industry."

NOEL (nodding eagerly): "The thing's got to be safer than my sister," he said. "And kinder."

BRAD: "Your sister?"

GIFF: "I never met her. Fatback won't share her telephone number."

NOEL: "That's for your own good."

GIFF: "Anyway, she's supposed to be a piece of work. The fabled great white cunt."

"Do you ever clear your debts?" Giff asked the next day when they were running alone.

"Why should I owe you money?" asked Noel, genuinely bewildered.

Giff smiled. "You've forgotten. I am entitled $100 the first time you get involved with anybody even remotely female."

"What if it doesn't last a month?" asked Noel.

"Why wouldn't it last a month?" Giff asked.

"We can't stand each other."

Giff nodded. "So you're saving yourself for something better?"

"That's right," said Noel.

"Good," said Giff. "Show's character." And then they ran in silence for a mile. "I suppose this sounds old-fashioned," Giff said, when they got back to the Y, "but I still think a chap should father his own illegitimate children."

Noel phoned Wilson that afternoon with a question about publicity for *Finding a Cure*. That evening they went to the one decent restaurant in Bedford Hills. Afterward they repaired to his apartment. "It's cute," she said, when Noel had unlocked the door. "The place cries out for plants, though. And carpeting."

By the time Noel connected with Giff again, it was in the middle of the following week. The editor sneaked out of his office early, went to the cash machine, took out five twenties.

Tuesday, August 27, 1985. I'm down to 147 pounds. Hotcha!

I reported my success to Giff. I expected him to be impressed. He wasn't impressed.

NOEL: "I think of women as being fattening."

GIFF: "You're such a rube. You never heard of pussy lite?"

15

THE SLIGHTLY
WHITE PAPERS

THURSDAY, SEPTEMBER 12, 1985. 9:35 A.M. Wilson is pregnant, so I have cravings. Up to 153 pounds. But then I did have a fever. And so needed to eat. Starve a cold and stuff a fever.

```
Fulton Basque Holloway
Holloway, Holloway & Stone
230 Benefit Street
Providence, Rhode Island 02903
```

Dearest Tony,

When Napoleon was a young man and frustrated with his career in France, he sent a letter to the British Admiralty applying for a position in England's armed forces. He was a Corsican, after all, and not necessarily loyal to the French. But imagine how history would have been altered if the English had accepted this particular applicant? And it's not as if they interviewed the future Emperor, and found him inadequate for a midshipman's berth. They didn't even bother to

answer the letter. And so, my friend, answering
letters is important. Unless you're secretly
writing that novel we've talked so much about,
it's your one great shot at fame, your one
chance to be immortal.

    Kat said you've been ill. A cold. Try
snacking. Stuff a cold and starve a fever.

Love,
No

P.S. Napoleon's genitals are said to be owned by
a prominent American urologist? He lives in
Westchester. My county. He also has the key to
Lincoln's box at the Ford Theater.

Friday, September 20, 1985. Still Another Great Reason for
Thinness: also culled from Jane Brody's seminal article, which
I've kept right here in my desk, for instructional readings. Along
with the story about my parents getting blown to bits in the
promised land. Anyway, "Dr. Edward J. Masoro, chairman of
the department of physiology at the University of Texas Health
Sciences Center at San Antonio, showed that cutting protein
intake in half significantly lengthened the lives of laboratory
rats."

    In other news, a deranged man cleaned out the showroom at a
Ford dealership outside of Boston. He broke in at lunchtime
wearing a Day-Glo ski mask and carrying a pump shotgun. He's
supposed to have wounded three people, killed one. This happened two days ago and already they've made him a phenome-
non and then a sort of hero. There were interviews with
sympathetic neighbors. His wife had just left him. He had a horrid childhood. "I never saw his father play catch with that boy.
Not once." We even got a video tour of the murderer's room,
with the soundtrack from *Taxi Driver* in the background.

He looks exactly like a guy Giff brought with us for a run. The one who quoted Alfred, Lord Tennyson at me. Can't be the same man. Too much of a coincidence. And yet the resemblance is uncanny. The killer has a two-point program. Point 1. He wants all products with the exception of those designed with fragility in mind—crystal or china, for instance—to pass the stronger-than-packaging test. In other words, if the carton is sturdier than the contents, that's no good. Yank the price tag off your new shirt, the shirt is ripped, the price tag remains intact, you get a full refund. Same with shrink wrap, same with the wires used to fasten children's toys to their cardboard cases.

Point 2. He wants the IRS regulations rewritten into a document no more than fifty pages long, and comprehensible to the average seven-year-old. If anyone is accused of violating an IRS regulation, then the taxpayer can go before a judge with any seven-year-old. If the seven-year-old can't explain the regulation clearly from what's written, the fine is thrown out, and the IRS actually owes the defendant the exact sum of money it was trying to collect.

Monday, September 23, 1985. It's 3 P.M. The exact time of day at which Christ died. Is this why I always feel blue in the afternoon? My palms itch, my sides ache. Giff has a "friend" named Kimberly coming in from Albany with her sister. Somebody is needed to distract the sister, while Giff and Kimberly renew acquaintance. The sister's name is Donna.

NOEL: "As in 'Oh Donna'?"

GIFF: "As in oh, oh, oh, oh Donna!" Giff wants us to go on a double date.

NOEL: "I'm too old to double-date."

GIFF: "Are not."

NOEL: "I was born too old to double-date. Besides, what about Wilson?"

GIFF: "I thought she was pregnant."

NOEL: "She is. But she's still my girl. What if she found out?"

GIFF: "Well I'm certainly not going to tell her. She still that hot? Got you exhausted?"

Actually, it's not that hot anymore, although I didn't tell this to Giff. Mostly we read. Lie beside each other in bed with books. She's reading *Decisive Battles of the World*. I'm reading *What to Expect When You're Expecting*.

———————————

Tuesday, September 24, 1985. Ran with Giff. He'd told Donna about me. "She's always wanted to be a writer. She's very excited. Will you do it?"

NOEL: "No."

Giff didn't say anything until we got back to the locker. "You a faggot or something?"

NOEL: "Or something, I guess. I like to fuck Wilson."

GIFF: "You'd probably also like to fuck Donna. I'm going to let you in on a little secret." Then he got off the tin stool on which he'd been sitting, came over, and whispered angrily into my ear. "They almost all of them have cunts."

That's what Philip Roth says. And I suppose he's looked. For all the girls I checked, though, a cunt may be a rare thing, like a goiter, or double-jointedness. Which makes the ones you do find all the more precious.

———————————

Two bombs went off last week in Idaho. Mail bombs. Each one was sent with a piece of a poem. One of the poems was by Wordsworth. The other was not by Wordsworth. Still, they've begun to call him or her the Wordsworth Bomber. Oddly, as the character of this personality begins to solidify, I'm finding

myself in sympathy. He reads poetry. He's against shoddy workmanship. What might I do in this world? I mean if I had the
courage of my convictions?

———————————

Thursday, September 26, 1985. I took the afternoon off so that I
could be with Wilson for the amnio. The needle is enormous. It
looks like something Bugs Bunny might use to give Elmer Fudd
a painful and unnecessary injection. When the doctor stuck it
into Wilson, I very nearly passed out. "Get your head down," he
yelled. I did, and was all right. He must've seen fainthearted husbands in his day.

Some nut opened fire at a McDonald's in San Ysidro, California. Killed twenty-one people. Many of them children. They
arrested him and it turns out that he wants them to reduce the
commercials on children's television by half. Also he wants the
actual consumers of products to be used in all television advertising. No actors, just real, actual people, picked at random. He
says that commercials with actors playing satisfied customers
are a form of deceit, and that they pollute public discourse.

In other, totally unrelated news, Tony has asked me to be his
best man. That's right, he's marrying my sister. Poor Polly. She
really loved that guy.

———————————

Friday, September 27, 1985. I always thought her handsome, but
now Wilson is even more compelling. Coming up stairs, or
through a doorway, she'll pause and take my arm, not as a hollow
courtesy, but because it's needed. God, what a wonderful feeling.
Her color is deeper, and she's developed a slow, stately gait, more
like an ocean liner than a girl.

Moving cheerfully along with *Finding a Cure: The True Story of
the Lily White Chemical Corporation.* Just last week the company's

most popular blood pressure drug was shown to cause impotence in "a significant number of male patients." Read most
male patients above the age of seven. Nancy brought me a copy
of the story. "I thought you should see this," she said. Then
Campbell showed up, stood casually in the doorway to my office.

"New take on that title," Campbell said. "Let's call it *Caveat
Emptor. Phallus Busters. The Slightly White Papers.*"

16

KNOWING IS FOR GOD

WEDNESDAY, OCTOBER 23, 1985. (155 lbs.) Lost some time again. What's the line from Pooh? "It doesn't really matter, if I don't get any fatter, and I don't get any fatter what I do." But I do get any fatter, what I do. Besides which, I think it does matter.

[Editor's note: What follows is cobbled together from interviews and from oblique references in the journals and from a conversation Noel had with his sister. Apparently, the incident described was so troubling that Noel was reluctant to examine it, or even record it. We do know that on Sunday afternoon October 27, 1985, Noel went to the Fox Lane High School track to run quarters.]

He had finished his workout and was just coming off the track when a canary yellow Subaru pulled into the lot. A young woman got out.

Noel was instantly taken with the woman, according to Kat, whom Noel spoke with that evening. "I'd guess it was partly the time of day," Noel told Kat. "She had a lanyard around her neck on which was hung a chrome stopwatch. This caught the last rays of the setting sun. She carried a black Nike gym bag with an orange swoosh. This she put down near the bleachers and began to run her own quarters. She would run a 440, then walk a 440, then run one. Noel told me he wanted to watch her for a bit. So he began to do his stretches against the first row of bleachers," Kat said.

"It was a good show, I guess," Kat said, "but he'd been running, he began to feel the colder air of evening." Apparently Noel walked to his car, switched on the engine, started out the drive to the main road. He was stopped at the traffic signal, waiting to make his left onto Route 117 when a great old clunker of a Ford swung off the main road and pulled into the parking lot behind the athletic field. There was a single man in the driver's seat. Noel told Kat the man didn't look like a runner. Nor did Noel think he looked like the woman's husband. "I had a hunch," he told his sister, "but I've had hunches."

Monday, October 28, 1985. Evening. Giff wasn't at the Y. I was relieved. My legs were too stiff for a hard run. I ran instead with Brad. Brad's not as fast as I am. But then he has got to be fifteen years my senior. He's about Campbell's age. He's still a good-looking man, gray around the temples and with a nicely proportioned face. Bushy eyebrows. Or did I already tell you that? He looks like a gentleman. Who but a gentleman would come up with the Cruise Hostess?

It started with Brad telling me how thirty years ago, he used to enjoy going out to pick up girls in a bar near a nursing school in a town forty miles from where he lived and went to high school. "I would borrow my father's truck. It had one of those speedometers which was easily disconnected. As long as I refilled the gas tank, he had no way of knowing how far I'd gone. I was big for my age. I was sixteen and could easily pass for eighteen. My friend and I both had fake IDs. The roads weren't good then and so it took a long time to make the drive. Also it was tough coming back, drunk. And we were young, not experienced drivers."

NOEL: "So why'd you do it?"

BRAD: "Nobody knew us there. We could tell them we were Harvard undergraduates. Sometimes I'd say I'd come home to visit my mother. If the girl was a melancholy, I told her I'd come home because my father had just died of a heart attack the day before. I'd tell her that it was difficult to get the time off from

school, what with the scholarship jobs and my being a class officer, but that everybody understood my need to take a couple of
days off, comfort my mother. I'd say that I was an only child. The
sad ones liked that a lot. If there was an awkward pause in the
conversation, I'd say I was thinking about my dead father."

NOEL: "Did they believe you?"

BRAD: "Mostly not."

NOEL: "So why'd you do it?"

BRAD: "When they did believe us—and it happened—we
always got laid. Always. I actually had one girl check us into a
motel and undress me. Use her own cash. That's how much she
wanted to help."

NOEL: "You are a shit."

BRAD: "That was a long time ago, but you know it wasn't
just the snatch. It was also knowing that I could be somebody
else. I liked that. Miss it."

NOEL: "I guess I know what you mean, I like sometimes to
be somebody else."

BRAD: "Example?"

NOEL: "Usually I have to be provoked."

BRAD: "Like when?"

NOEL: "Last night I took the very pregnant girlfriend out to
a Jeff Bridges movie and then to a new French restaurant in
Scarsdale. (One star.)

[Editor's Note: Stars are harder to come by in Westchester.]

I'm in the bathroom, at the urinal and this guy comes in, goes to
the urinal beside me. I was wearing chinos and a polo shirt. He
was in a full suit, better dressed than I. He looked me up and
down. I could tell he was wondering how I was going to afford
this restaurant. Which he might well have wondered since right
then I too was wondering how I could afford this restaurant.
Without saying anything, he gave the impression that he was
looking down on me, or at least he was looking away from my

fiscal and sumptuary embarrassment. So I struck up a conversation. I said that the older I got, the less I liked the cold. He dïdn't like the winter either, but he said he hated the early spring worst of all. So I said that if he hated the spring, he must be an accountant. So he said he was an accountant. He didn't figure me for an accountant, though. He thought I must be a lawyer. I could tell here that he was shooting high, trying to flatter me, since I looked more like a housepainter or a gardener than a lawyer. I said, no, that I wasn't a lawyer. I said I was a brain surgeon."

BRAD: "A brain surgeon?"

NOEL: "I told him that my name was Frederick Hollenzollern (no relation to the Prussian dynasty) and that I operated out of an office on Park Avenue. I said I'd been called to the hospital for an emergency, which is why my clothes were crumpled. He wanted to know if I liked the work."

BRAD: "What did you tell him?"

NOEL: "By this time I was washing my hands. I told him that what bothered me was that there never seemed to be enough time to speak with the patients and their families. I said that while it was imperative to be an excellent surgeon, I thought it almost equally important to make the effort to be with the people who were impacted by the disease, speak with them, allay their fears."

BRAD: "You said that?"

NOEL: "I said I supposed I could earn additional monies if I scheduled more operations, but I preferred to take on fewer people and make absolutely certain I had the time to handle the emotional side of every single case. I said that for instance the woman I was dining with was a widow. I said that her husband, an advertising executive, had just died in an operation performed by one of my junior colleagues, and I was taking her out to dinner, just to keep her from being alone with her loss. 'She can't date, you know,' I said, and made a motion with my arms to indicate pregnancy.

"He said that this must be awkward. I said not really, because she played cello for the New York Philharmonic, and so we were spending the evening discussing classical music. I smiled and went out of the bathroom. My girlfriend and I finished dinner and the waiter appeared with cognac."

BRAD: "It was from the man you'd met at the urinal."

NOEL: "That's right. He came over, very apologetic about disturbing us. He said that he and his wife had spent the whole of dinner discussing me. He said his wife had wanted to meet me. I stood and we all shook hands. Then he said, that if—God forbid—he ever had any trouble with his brain, I'd be the guy he went to."

After the run, I stopped at Zaro's, waited on line for a cinnamon raisin bagel with cream cheese and a can of seltzer. The woman at the register actually said, "Is that all?" She said it, not me. So, once I'd paid, I went around the corner and bought a small vanilla frozen yogurt. The bagel was cut in half. Back at the office, I took it apart, wrapped the larger section in one of two napkins and put it into my wastebasket. I ate my frozen yogurt. I ate the small half of the bagel. I drank my can of seltzer. Then I fished the large half of the bagel out of the wastebasket. I ate that, too.

That evening Noel met 4C in the stairwell. Mrs. Whiting is a woman in her midsixties. "I never liked him," she explained to us, when we spoke with her. "He used to try to play the harmonica. Such a klutz. I asked him if he'd heard of the Orsini girl."

"Who's the Orsini girl?" Noel asked.

"I thought you were a runner."

"I am a runner."

"She's always in the local papers. She won the Westchester Half Marathon. You must have seen her."

"I don't follow the running news."

"Poor woman was killed two days ago. She was up at the track at some high school. I think it's Fox Lane. Near 684."

"That's Fox Lane," said Noel.

Mrs. Whiting nodded. "They caught the man who did it."

"Wait a minute," said Noel, pulling away. "What does she drive? Is it a Subaru?"

"I don't know what she drives," said Mrs. Whiting. And she told us, she didn't know what he was getting at. "Poor, dear woman," she said. "Now there are two small children without a mother."

Noel just wagged his head.

"At least they arrested him," said Mrs. Whiting. "Some out-of-work housepainter. He used to date her in high school. Never got over her. Or the army."

"Has he spoken yet to the press?" Noel asked. "Taken any positions?"

Noel's neighbor was at first confused by this question, and then annoyed. "I thought I'd misheard him," she told us. But I hadn't. "Why should he have a position? He's a murderer, that's all. A rapist."

"I just wondered," Noel told her. "Nowadays most of them do."

Tuesday, October 29, 1985. I told Giff about having been there right before the rape. Asked him if I should call the police now that the murderer has already confessed. Giff agreed that I should stay out of it.

NOEL: "So I'm not doing anything wrong?"

GIFF: "Legally, you are obligated to come forward. But as long as you weren't seen."

NOEL: "I mean morally. I'm not doing anything wrong morally?"

GIFF: "Not now, you're not."

NOEL: "Or the day before the day before yesterday?"

GIFF (reaching out and touching his friend's shoulder affectionately): "Actually, you might have gone back. You might have saved her life."

NOEL: "If I'd turned around, he wouldn't have attacked her. I would not have known if I'd done the right thing."

GIFF (shrugging): "What made you suspicious?"

NOEL: "A hunch really. And the car. It was a big old American car."

GIFF: "Like the one you drive?"

NOEL: "That's right."

We ran in silence for a while. I was watching my friend's face for signs of condemnation. "It's never a matter of knowing," Giff said, finally. "You guess. Then you act. Then you try to forgive yourself. Knowing is for God. Didn't your father ever tell you that?"

6:11 P.M. In totally unrelated news, I'm gaining weight. I'm up to 156 pounds. If it's a boy, Nicolaus or Alexander. A girl will be Sophie or Amanda.

17

HOMEWARD BOUND

Fulton Basque Holloway
Holloway, Holloway & Stone
230 Benefit Street
Providence, Rhode Island 02903
Thursday, January 2, 1986

Tony:

   I'm desolate that Wilson couldn't come. I
would have loved to have the two of you meet. I
thought you looked great, so stern and
committed. Proud to have been your best man.
Gorgeous wife you've chosen. Is danger always
part of beauty, I wonder?
   I'm not married, but we are pregnant. I've
spent a lot of time shopping for the unborn.
Which is more fattening than quitting smoking. I
shopped for the layette. I paid for the layette.
I noticed that none of the other men looked too
chipper either, a bunch of shamefaced bulls. We
all hang over our belts, we none of us hang
below.

I've never been to prison, but I have been to
jail, and a man in jail looks about 100 percent
better than a man pricing changing tables. In
jail you can rattle your bars. At Darling
Discount Juvenile Furniture in White Plains, you
are expected to beam and coo.

Love,
No

Katherine Moses Holloway

c/o Fulton Basque Holloway
Holloway, Holloway & Stone
230 Benefit Street
Providence, Rhode Island 02903

                                    Sunday, January 12, 1986

Dear Kat,

You were a splendid bride. Practically
virginal. The present beneath his Christmas
tree. And now you've become an aunt.

No, there's no consanguinity, but I do feel
very fatherly. Thursday, January 9, it actually
happened. A red-letter day. Eight pounds and
three ounces. Complete with hair, which the
doctor says will fall out and fingernails, which
the doctor says will fall out. And a belly
button, which the doctor says will fall off.

I'm afraid I didn't make much of a contribu-
tion during the delivery, despite extensive
training in Lamaze. Unless you count standing

around holding a tennis ball looking awkward,
while the woman you adore writhes in mortal
pain. I thought she was going to die. She
thought she was going to die. Everything
came out just fine. Apparently this always
happens.

I've been staying in Connecticut, taking the
2 A.M. and 5 A.M. feedings. Then Wilson and I
ride the same train into Grand Central. We don't
sit together. She says she's had it up to here--
finger to throat--with domesticity.

Love,
No

P.S. Tell your husband to write his best friend
a letter.

But Tony didn't write to Noel. And our quarry goes completely off the
record for almost eight months. It is as if he ceased to exist. No letters,
no journal entries. Amelia Bishop reported that he was out of the office
a lot. "Which is odd," she said. "Considering his increased responsibilities." George Peabody reports that Hammersmith rarely appeared
at the Y.

Giff couldn't remember anything either. "He was gaining weight," he
told us. "Of that much I'm certain. And there used to be puke stains
sometimes on the left shoulder of his suit jacket."

The bombings stopped.

Katherine Moses Holloway
c/o Fulton Basque Holloway
Holloway, Holloway & Stone
230 Benefit Street
Providence, Rhode Island 02903

Friday, July 11, 1986

Dear Kat,

I'm writing just to you from now on. The
lawyer never writes back.

Wilson (she's the woman I love) had a series
of conferences Saturday. I put the baby seat in
the Chevrolet (the heartbeat of America) and we
went to the playground. We sat in the sandbox. I
tried to read, Bart tried to eat sand. I managed
to keep him from eating a lot of sand. He
managed to keep me from doing a lot of reading.

Every so often we'd break for a baby joke. I
pick him up by the armpits, hold him way over my
head: "Ever hear the one about the farmer's
daughter?" Then I lower him and blow farting
noises onto his bare stomach. Bart laughs and
laughs. He thinks I'm a gifted humorist.

Being around the kid reminds me of Dad.
Remember mother didn't like to drive? So Dad did
most of the errands. Before you were born, he
used to take me around.

I take Bart around. We stopped at the
stationery store. I got myself some sugarless
bubble gum, and for his Highness a helium
balloon. From there we went to Caldor's. I put
the infant seat in the shopping cart, tied the
balloon to the handle.

I couldn't locate the Fisher-Price car seat
Wilson wanted. I bought tube socks for myself,
and for Bart I picked out a copy of Horton
Hatches the Egg, marked way down. Or at least I
thought it was marked way down. Had a price tag

on it said $7.99 and price reduction. In the car
I scraped it off, and there was another price
tag said $6.99. So they must have reduced it
up $1.

When we got back to the apartment, I left
Bart alone with the balloon, while I dashed down
to the basement and put my running clothes in
the wash. He was crying when I came back
upstairs. Somehow he'd popped the balloon.
Crisis passed, we spread out together on the
floor. I read; Bart climbed on my stomach. I
don't know if he enjoyed it. I certainly did. "I
meant what I said, and I said what I meant, an
elephant's faithful 100 percent." I can't wait
until he gets old enough for Pooh. Or <u>The Bat
Poet</u>:

"A bat is born
Naked blind and pale."

A bat, on the other hand, grows out of it.

At five I heated a jar of lamb with broth
(no salt), and one of creamed spinach (also
no salt). The great advantage to baby food is
that it tastes dreadful. So I'm not tempted to
eat any myself. Feeding Bart is no fun, but at
least it's not fattening. I suspect that baby
food used to be delicious. Some killjoy took
it to a lab. Then he told the mothers that the
food had a lot of salt in it, plus sugar and
free radicals. Whatever they are. The manufacturers made their mush healthy. Which pleased
the mothers a lot. They don't have to eat the
stuff.

Bart throws his hands up as if I were trying
to murder him with the spoon. It's like
threading a needle, getting ground lamb into
that mouth. When I give up, I scrape most of
what's left out of the jars and leave them on
the counter. Wilson will think he's had a big
dinner. "Peanut never eats that well at home,"
she coos. Sometimes, if he really is hungry, I'll
boil a hot dog. You'd be astonished how easy it
is to get a hot dog into that tiny mouth.

Mayzie the Lazy Bird didn't show up until
7 P.M. "Early conference call tomorrow," she
said, and wrapped Bart in his traveling blanket.
I strapped the lad in place and the Volvo drove
off into the night.

Times like this, I long for a cigarette.
Something to do with my hands. Dad smoked
Camels. Do you envy him his cigarettes? In those
days a man could drink martinis, smoke Camels,
and still go right to heaven.

Love, No

PS: I suppose it's a requirement of his profession, but the old man did have a sense that the
world was well oiled. Life was running toward
paradise on tracks. Wordsworth was his favorite
poet, but remember he read Melville's White
Jacket once a year, in the spring. He loved to
quote the couplet with which that novel ends.

"Whoever afflict us, whatever surround,
Life is a voyage that's homeward bound!"

18

THE HAIR STAYED

SATURDAY, JULY 12, 1986. I just got off the phone with Che. "As a writer I've been out of commission for months now," he said. "Indian Point." I was tempted to say something about him never having been in commission, actually. But I didn't. I said I'd been out of commission, too. With a kid. Bartholomew Wilson. I don't think he got the joke. He didn't even ask for an explanation. Man has wooden ears. He's got the wind up about the TWA hijacking in Syria. Apparently, after the thirty-nine American hostages were freed, two of the Shiite terrorists boasted to reporters of "the ability of the oppressed to control America."

There was a bombing report in yesterday's paper. Che mentioned that, too. There have been seventeen deaths. Che was right about one thing. The Brooks Brothers incident is now acknowledged to have been the result of an explosive device.

Giff has taken to calling me Mr. Mom. He's only met Wilson once. She hated him. He hated her. He told me he doesn't even think she's gorgeous.

"She's gorgeous all right," I said. And I mean it. But then I've never been in love with a girl who didn't seem gorgeous at the time.

When we're out with people, my own true love is apt to look annoyed, as if my presence were inevitable but still unwelcome, as if I were a troublesome younger brother. She's quite different when we're alone. If we're going into my bedroom, she'll walk in front. Then when I come up behind her, she'll fall against my chest. I catch her under the arms. She cranes her neck backward and we kiss. Then she goes completely limp; I lift her onto the bed.

Out in the world, overdressed and with all that hair and moxie, one gets the impression that this is quite a lot of person. When she relaxes, though, W is surprisingly small. Easy to carry. I take her clothes off. I will kiss her on the throat. "Fuck me," she says. Her little body smells and tastes of talcum powder.

I must be essentially conventional because I almost always wind up on top of her at first. She gives a little ladylike grunt of satisfaction as it goes in. I kiss her on the forehead. She has this great, white neck. I kiss her there. I kiss her on the tops of her breasts. She'll take my hand and push it hard up against the base of her left breast, and then sigh. "Oh," she says, "Oh, No, Oh, No, Oh, No."

I understand Giff's confusion. If you saw W on the street, or met her at cocktail party, you probably wouldn't notice what a deep bosom she has. Often, she's in a double-breasted suit. She looks like a very young, slightly top-heavy businessman with terribly long hair. Used to be a certain kind of woman got herself up to look like a Prohibition gangster's moll. Now they dress like the gangster himself.

Get W out of those dreadful clothes, and she's packing a different sort of heat. We're in a biosphere, with the hair coming all the way down on either side. When it's over, I kiss her on the lips. These are cold as ice.

I have reason to believe that I don't measure up to her other lovers. The second or third time we fucked, she rolled off me and she was muttering, as if to the ceiling. "You know the missionary is not the only position," she said. "One orgasm doesn't need to be the circus." I'm still afraid to ask what she meant. I imagine that Bart's father was a red hot ticket. Not much for the Gerber hour, but nimble and tireless at night.

I don't complain. Usually, a guy meets a girl, he thinks she's thin. She gets up, or moves away from the potted plant she's been standing beside and it turns out she's got fat hips. Even if she is thin, they get involved and she'll grow large, or dull, or both.

I had the exact opposite experience. I met this girl with gorgeous auburn hair that fell to her waist. She had a fat tummy. I fell deeply in love. Now she has hardly any belly at all. The hair stayed.

19

PUTTING ON AIRS

THURSDAY, AUGUST 7, 1986. The instructor for the four-hour, $350-per-couple how-to-save-your-baby course wore a push dagger on the back of his belt. He told us that the knife—a Pocket Panther—has a serrated blade. This is for cutting people out of their safety belts. "You'd be surprised how many people are killed by those things."

A brave woman asked if safety belts weren't supposed to be, "You know, good for us?"

"They are," he said, and chuckled dryly. "Unless the car is stalled on the tracks, or on fire, or you've driven into deep water."

He wore high-heeled cowboy boots, stonewashed black jeans, and those mirrored sunglasses which I have always seen as an act of aggression. When he's not teaching parents how to restart the infant heart, he drives ambulances. He seems much more interested in taking lives than in saving them. He kept telling us stories about dead babies, mutilated babies. "Just a couple of months ago, I got called to a residence in Riverdale. Ever been to Riverdale?"

Some of us had.

"Nice home." He said and wagged his head sadly. "The woman didn't know what had hit her." The little girl—an only child— had been playing with a helium balloon. It popped. The kettle whistled, and the mother went into the kitchen to turn off the Garland stove. "You wouldn't believe the size of the range," he told us, spreading his arms apart. "Like from a restaurant. Anyway, it was the Nanny's day off. Poor lady had to make her own tea." This got a chuckle. "By the time she returned to the playroom the kid had the balloon popped and the rubber wad caught in her throat." He paused. "Now I'm going to show you what to do about choking."

I raised my hand.

INSTRUCTOR: "What?"

NOEL: "The girl?"

INSTRUCTOR (shrugging): "We did a trache. But it was too late."

NOEL (incredulous): "Killed by a balloon?"

INSTRUCTOR: "Not dead actually, brain dead. Probably never talk, or walk unassisted. She'll live, though."

This got an appreciative sigh from the class.

INSTRUCTOR: "Don't laugh. It happens. Babies often choke. It should be against the law to leave a small child alone with a balloon," he said reminding me of having recently left a child alone with a balloon. Hot dogs (Bart's favorite) are lethal, carrots, grapes, pretzels, macaroni. Then there are electric cords to bite through, stairs to fall down, swimming pools to tumble into. Infant seats can slip off of high places. "That heavy Mexican tile that's recently come into fashion, it's as hard as stone. Crack an infant's skull like an eggshell." Kitchen cabinets are stocked with poison; a surprising number of common house plants have toxic leaves and berries.

After a cursory and mostly unhelpful series of demonstrations, we were all given dolls to practice our lifesaving techniques on. The dolls were little girls. They didn't have bras, but they did have underpants. I was supposed to save my miniature cheesecake from drowning. When the instructor came by, I was earnestly blowing air into her throat. "You're doing that exactly wrong," he said, and stalked off.

That's good, I thought. *Now at least I'll be confident.*

Afterward, in the cab we shared downtown, Wilson wouldn't talk. She was on her way to Soho for a dinner with clients. Plan was, I'd leave the cab at Grand Central, catch the train to Bedford Hills. After I'd gotten out, she let me kiss her on the cheek. "I suppose I was the worst one in the class," I said.

"Bullshit," she said. "Don't put on airs!"

20

LET THE BOY FIGURE
IT OUT FOR HIMSELF

President
Gerber Baby Foods
Freemont, Michigan
Sunday, September 21, 1986

To Whom It May Concern:

You say that babies are your business--your
only business, but the stuff you vend for them
to eat is horrid. Tasteless. And I know. Because
I've tasted it.

In the past, I have gotten around this
problem by feeding my son more conventional
foods, chopped hot dogs, carrots, grapes.
Recently I was told that many children choke to
death on hot dogs. What one really should feed a
child is mush, but if the mush is entirely
without flavor, they won't eat it.

I think I know how this has happened. With
the new interest in low-sodium, low-fat foods,
the mothers are reading the labels. So you
took the salt and sugar out of the jar. But
what's the use of compelling labels if the food

tastes like landfill? You've mistaken form for
substance. I, personally, was brought up with a
lofty opinion of corporate responsibility. When
my father, an Episcopalian minister, was a young
man, he once bought a box of Cracker Jack's, and
discovered that the prize was missing. He wrote
to the president of the Cracker Jack company,
and was sent a note of apology, which was so
compelling that my father kept it framed behind
the desk in the rectory.

Sincerely,
Noel Hammersmith

Friday, November 21, 1986. I got a postcard from Che. It's a picture of a musket. On the back he wrote, "My Life stood like a
loaded gun." Isn't that Emily Dickinson? Blue morning, and
couldn't figure out why. I went for my noon run, came back, and
looked at the paper. Now I know why I'm depressed. We're cele-
brating the anniversary of the Kennedy assassination. It's Lee
Harvey Oswald Day. Kids learn as much about Lee Harvey
Oswald as they do about George Washington. George Washington led a victorious rebel army, refused a kingdom. Oswald used
to hit Marina. All of which is forgotten. He's a great mystery.
He's a great man. All you need, all you really need for immortal-
ity nowadays is a cold eye and a mail-order rifle.

Thursday, December 11, 1986. They are talking seriously now
about turning the Lord & Lady Ampleworth Apartments into a
co-op. This means I will be "encouraged" to make a big payment
in order to live here. All the money I have is in savings. But

maybe if I buy the apartment, put the rest in the market, that will grow and I'll break even.

Che sent me a piece of a manuscript and a column clipped from *Newsday* speculating about the possibilities of terrorism in this country. "A single, super-intelligent and highly motivated individual can significantly alter the destiny of a nation." What, I wonder, is why do they always assume these people are superintelligent? Isn't it ever possible for a sociopath to be a sleepwalker? Or an oaf?

The manuscript is what Archer Peabody used to call a set piece. It's—you guessed it—Christmas Eve in Grand Central Station. There's a high school glee club belting carols, weary parents laden with packages are lining up at Zaro's to buy a last cup of coffee before catching the train home. Meanwhile, there's a bomb in the wastebin right near Zaro's. Che claims that the foreign terrorists would want to strike over the holidays, hit at the heart of the Christian year. Trouble is, I have no idea how he knows this. Or even if he knows this.

December 27, 1986. This Christmas Bart got the train set. Lionel. (The trains that railroad men buy for their boys.) Wilson wouldn't let me plug it in, though. She's terrified the junior engineer will be electrocuted. I thought he'd leave it here, in my apartment, and I could play with it. But Bart wanted to take it home. And I don't blame him, really. Although I was curious to see if the little engine actually does blow smoke.

In totally unrelated news I'm up to 170 pounds. Tubaluba. Lard Ass. Fatback.

Saturday, January 10, 1987. So busy with bottles and nappies that I've completely lost track of time. I'm writing today because yesterday was Bart's first birthday. Wilson was the sexy mother, in scarlet floor-length evening gown with diving cleavage. In fact she had what looked like a hickey on her left shoulder. If it is a hickey, I don't remember having had anything to do with it. "A pimple, silly," she said.

Bart loves the fire engine I gave him. This is one of those toys on wheels that toddlers push around, so that they can walk behind it, when ordinarily they don't know how. It's a bright red hook and ladder in hard plastic. He stands behind the contraption with this grotesquely serious look on his face, his socks much longer than his feet and he pushes it over the floor. When he runs into a wall, he shrieks. Then he screams. Then he cries. I pull him out and point him toward open floor. Wilson thinks I should back off. "Let the boy figure it out for himself," she says.

21

A COBRA IN THE
SUPPLY CLOSET

THURSDAY, JANUARY 15, 1987. (189 lbs.) 5 P.M. In office. Big news, but first let's get the business out of the way. I'm going to buy the co-op. Put every nickel left in the stock market. Where it will grow. Ensure my golden years. I even have a broker. Wilson gave him to me. Along with the lawyer for the closing. Broker's name is Bigg. "Jeff Bigg with two g's." But now the big news. Big with one g. I'll tell it as it happened. Strengthen the dramatic muscle.

First I heard sounds out on the hallway. Little muffled shrieks. I asked Amelia to shut my door. Which she did. Nancy didn't even knock, went right past Amelia, burst into my sanctuary. This was at about 10 A.M. She took my right arm in both of her hands. "Come, come." Her glasses were crooked, but she didn't seem to be hurt. She brought me into the hallway.

They were all in a line, looking at the wall. The shoulders and behind of a messenger, I could tell by the uniform. The back and shoulders of a woman I know from production. I could tell by the fat ankles. Campbell's back. I could just tell. And then somebody so small that at first I thought this might be a daughter, up to visit her mother's office.

Nancy still had me by the arm, and pulled me through the line, right up to an empty Kleenex box which had been propped up against the wall. I said, "Am I supposed to guess?" Nobody laughed. Nobody even spoke. So I leaned forward. I picked up the box. There was a mouse under there, not clockwork, but real. Flesh and blood. Poor sucker was sitting trembling, too frightened even to make a mess.

"Booh," I said. The mouse skittered down the hall and went under the door to the supply closet.

I straightened, turned to look at my audience. I could see the girl from the front now, but she wasn't a girl. She was just a very small woman. Remember Green Eyes? It's her. Green Eyes. I guess she's not an heiress on account of she's just taken a job here in our company, in public relations. We did a little dance back and forth. "I know you," I said. "And I know you," she said and twinkled.

Meanwhile Nancy was wondering if I'd made the mouse angry. "He's cornered now," she said. "When cornered, even a mouse will fight."

I got the distinct impression that Nancy had wanted me to murder the mouse, like Orwell in *To Shoot an Elephant,* only on a different scale obviously.

"I think it's a rat," I said.

"Small for a rat," said Nancy.

"Not the animal, the quote. If cornered, even a rat will fight."

"Oh," said Nancy. "Rat or mouse, I'm not going into that supply closet again. Ever!" So we agreed that everybody should calm down. Everybody should go back to work. And that from this day forward, I will be the one who goes into the supply closet.

NANCY: "Even for pencils?"

NOEL "Even for pencils."

WOMAN FROM PRODUCTION: "Cross your heart."

NOEL: "I cross my heart."

Then Green Eyes came and stood in front of me, very close, well within my privacy zone. (See *Privacy Zone: Gestures, Distances, and What They Mean,* Acropolis Books, 1983.) I could feel her breath. Then she took the big finger of my right hand and moved it against my chest. "I cross my heart, I hope to die, stick a needle in my eye," she said. It was a wonderful thing, the warmth of her hand on mine. Positive to positive; negative to ground.

Her name's not Green Eyes, of course. It's Fay. She followed me into my new big office. Turns out she's really very interested in being an editor. "But you didn't have any editorial jobs posted." Turns out that she and her husband have broken up.

NOEL: "He *was* enormous."

FAY: "Size wasn't the problem."

I told her I'd be glad to give her editorial work, as long as she kept up a presence in public relations. She thanked me a lot.

And that wasn't the end of it either. I met her a second time, later in the day. I was out on a solitary expedition. Deep in the treacherous supply closet. Looking for a legal pad.

FAY (looking startled): "I only needed envelopes. I thought you were busy."

NOEL: "Always busy, never too busy for a friend."

FAY: "You were great this morning."

NOEL: "Thanks."

FAY: "I guess this makes me an old-fashioned girl, but I believe in heroes."

NOEL: "If anybody deserves a medal here, it's the mouse. Thirty-seven floors. In the middle of Manhattan."

FAY: "Still. You were so, how to put it? . . . commanding."

NOEL: "Mice I can handle. I understand them. Don't call me when there's a cobra in the supply closet."

22

THE LAW OF CONTRARY

MONDAY, JANUARY 19, 1987. Tollah's been fired. He was my mentor. I would have gone to see him, but apparently he cleared out before they even made the announcement. Campbell says he thinks there might actually have been criminal charges. "I know the FBI came up here twice to speak with him."

They've brought in somebody named Andrew Layman to replace Tollah. He's fat and bald. And wears bad suits. At least Tollah was handsome. Layman's coming to us from a big potato chip company. He says that if he can sell potato chips, then he can certainly sell books. He says it'll be easier. "Books have a much longer shelf life." Enough to make me long for our helicopter pilot. Oh, and Layman has already made a change. Where the slogan used to be Acropolis: Best Little Publishing House in America, now it's going to be Acropolis: Best Little Publishing House in the World.

I asked Campbell, "How does he know that?"

CAMPBELL: "He doesn't."

Tuesday, January 20, 1987. Fay was at my desk when I got in this morning at 8:15 A.M. Well before official hours begin at nine. She was wearing one of those dresses that looks exactly like a very long T-shirt. A very long T-shirt that has been squirted with a hose. This was green. She had it cinched at the waist with a thick black belt. She's tiny, and perfect in every detail. Statuesque. A statuette.

And well spoken. She's been teaching at community colleges. "I got so far away from the material. Just keeping the students awake was a challenge."

She got bored with the academic world. She thinks she'll clear her sinuses with the purer fires of capitalism. She's an adventuress and wants to walk on the wild side, out near the bottom line. She told me the whole story. "I used to write poetry. Discovered men. Gave up poetry. Now that I've spent some time with men, I think maybe the poetry was better than it had seemed at the time."

She's in public relations, officially (did I already tell you this?) but wants to know if she can work in editorial during her lunch break. "Then if you have an opening. . . ." I walked over to the sofa which is heaped with manuscripts and gave her three of the least promising. You think this is ungenerous? Remember the cowboy hat, the knives, the broken chess set. I know, I know, she didn't do it. But if it hadn't been for her sudden and wrenching appearance, I might well have called MasterCard a week before I did. I might have saved hundreds of dollars, plus the heartache.

She reappeared at noon with a cup of Dutch Apple yogurt. She asked if I was going for a run. I was going for a run. Could she eat in my office? Certainly she could eat in my office. Could she sit at my desk? Certainly she could sit at my desk.

Dutch Apple yogurt has more than 200 calories, maybe 220 calories. When I buy yogurt I always get the plain, which has only 150 calories. Then I put fake sugar in it. That's four calories for a total of 154.

ANOTHER GREAT REASON FOR THINNESS: You can eat fattening foods.

Wednesday, January 21. Fay came by today after work. I see more of her nowadays than I do of Wilson. But I'm still Wilson's creature. She needs me. Bart needs me. I wouldn't endanger that for any other set of eyes. However green.

Wilson's out tonight for business and has hired a nanny. So I wasn't in a hurry to get home. Fay interviewed me. I used to interview people when I worked at the newspaper, but I've never had it done to me. She didn't take notes, but seemed almost to have prepared her questions in advance.

She's doing profiles of all the editors for a new catalogue we're considering. Layman thinks personality is important in marketing.

I found the whole process quite flattering. She's so kind, so intense. Fay wanted to know the history of my alphabet series. Which is widely considered my most brilliant work.

NOEL: "It all started off with *H Is for Hemorrhoid*. Most men get to be thirty years old, they get piles. They bleed, they worry. They're too humiliated to admit their condition to one another, and too stingy to see a doctor. So we had this little book, with a cover that played down the title. Still sells a few thousand copies a year. We've also had *M Is for Micturate*. We get the very young hooked with *P Is for Premature Ejaculation*. *I Is for Impotence* sells on the other end of the age curve. I'm getting a proposal soon on *R Is for Regularity*."

Thursday, January 22, 1987. Ran with Giff and Tom at noon. Tom seems interested in me, which is odd, since I'm not at all sure he likes me. I like him. Tom's a pleasure to look at, handsome and serious and still. The exact opposite of Pig. Pig is always talking about his values, which leaves me with the suspicion that perhaps he has none. The law of contrary.

23

SOMEBODY ELSE'S
HALLWAYS

TUESDAY, FEBRUARY 3, 1987. (190 lbs.) The executive board met yesterday. Campbell and I went down to 36. This was my maiden visit to the new boardroom. Ever notice that when a corporation is getting ready to fire people, they first always refurbish all the executive facilities? Anyway, I found the fabulous setup to be quite the little disappointment. It does have one of those big shiny pieces of black wood that they've been using a lot of Endust on. But there were no silver carafes of coffee, no microphones. Just some men who don't much like each other sitting around a table that's too big to eat on, and the wrong shape for Ping-Pong.

The big news is that Layman wants Fay fired.

NOEL: "Whatever for?"

LAYMAN: "She's new. She's still on probation. She's not doing her work."

NOEL: "She's interested in editorial, actually."

LAYMAN: "So then is she doing your work?"

NOEL: "Not yet, but she's made a good start."

LAYMAN: "How much time will it take to see if she can function as an editor?"

NOEL: "A couple of years."

LAYMAN: "You've got six months. She'd better also find time to do her day job."

NOEL: "It takes a while to cultivate a writer, get him going, and known by the public."

Campbell chuffed a couple of times but said nothing. Since Archer Peabody left, Campbell's been doing our chuffing for us.

LAYMAN (to me): "You like her, right?"

NOEL: "Yes, I suppose."

LAYMAN: "I like her, too. But this isn't a finishing school. Besides which, there's no law against firing small people. Or not yet. So we'd better get in under the wire. She's got six months. After that she can go wag her tiny butt in somebody else's hallways."

24

TANT MIEUX!

WEDNESDAY, FEBRUARY 4, 1987. Dr. Franklin English is a cardiologist, and I don't know if he's fat, but he's blessedly brief. The manuscript is only 180 pages. Triple spaced. We're supposed to sell it with a blue plastic pyramid. The book is to be called *The Pyramid Diet*. The pyramid is three inches tall and opened at the bottom. You can follow a specific menu, with recipes for steamed broccoli and water chestnuts dusted with meat tenderizer, or you can eat anything you want, provided, of course, that in any twenty-four-hour period you don't put away more than can be stuffed into your blue plastic pyramid. You want to fill the pyramid with granulated sugar, you can do that. You want to fill it with cyanide, you can do that, too.

This is perfect for Fay. I was a little bit embarrassed, though, making the handoff. The plastic pyramid had a hole in it and was attached to the manuscript with a yellow plastic loop.

FAY: "A joke?"

NOEL: "No, not exactly."

FAY: "Your next project?"

NOEL: "I was hoping you'd make it yours."

Monday March 2, 1987. (193 lbs.) I read an article in *Redbook* yesterday while waiting for Wilson to have her hair done. This woman had written something down every day for a year. She lost twenty-two pounds. It's true, you know, that many writers are slender. I thought it was because they were poor, or alcoholics who had stopped eating meals, but actually there may be some connection between thinness and self-expression. To eat today I've had one Zaro's muffin (bran). Yes, it was big. But it was also bran; reputed to be fat free. One Delicious apple (90 calories), one medium vanilla frozen yogurt (130), two bran cookies (80) and one banana (the perfect food). Oh, and six cups of coffee with milk and sugar. Refined sugar. "Only 16 calories per level teaspoon."

Saw a spread in the back of *Parade* for a diet kit. Pills you're suppose to take. I'm so desperate now that I actually wrote in for the catalogue.

I ran with Giff. He finds my relationship with Wilson bewildering in the extreme.

GIFF: "You don't have to say the words. Just nod. She's a virtuoso in bed, right?"

I shook my head.

GIFF: "She has a twin sister who shows up, Friday nights. Together they reenact all the most spectacular sex scenes from *The Arabian Nights*?"

NOEL: "Nope."

GIFF: "All right then, what is it?"

NOEL (shrugging): "I don't know."

GIFF: "Guess."

NOEL: "I'm fat. Fatsters can't be choosers." Not what I thought, though. What I thought was, she needs me. They both do.

Tuesday, March 3, 1987. (193 lbs.) I'm reading over a manuscript. *Imagine Yourself a Sylph* is the working title. It's by Dr.

Martin Roan, whom I happen to know buys his suits in the Portly Man section at Paul Stuart.

Roan wants you to close the door. Turn off the phone. Sit in a chair, or lie on a bed and picture a still pond at twilight. A single duck cuts across the evening sky. The sun sets. The moon is a silver slipper. "I am a still pond," you tell yourself as you breathe in. "I am a deep, still pond," you think, breathing out. Count each exhalation.

After twenty breaths out, you are instructed to draw up pictures of everything you've had to eat or drink during the previous twenty-four hours. As you think of each item, you imagine yourself putting it on your head. Cookies, for instance, would be crumbled up and mashed into the scalp. Hot chocolate and coffee with milk are to be poured. The beverages run down the sides of your face, in under your collar, puddle in your shoes. A footnote warns that you must include diet food, "because all comestibles [nice word], caloric and noncaloric, are feeding the monster within."

There's something unequivocal about a doctor's prose. They use the authority of their profession to establish an orthodoxy. Sometimes, as in the case of Dr. Stillman, the dieter is encouraged to eat hamburger patties. Other times, as in the case of Dr. Pritikin, hamburger patties are the last thing the dieter should eat. Most of the doctors would have you drink ten glasses of water every day. This is supposed to assuage your hunger. Makes perfect sense, right? When in the presence of a loud noise, cover your eyes.

Friday, March 6, 1987. (194 lbs.) I finished a rough cut of Roan's book, passed it on to Fay. I wanted her to look at it, get some feeling for how a line-edit might work. "Take out an additional hundred pages," I told her. "Diet doctors are fat. Diet books needn't be."

I got the booklet from the Golden Rule Vitamin people. Turns out we get fat because we build up gunk in our small intestines. So when we eat, the food can't go right into the bloodstream. So we're still hungry. So we eat more, get fat. The pills this company sells slough the gunk off our small intestines. That way when you eat something, you're immediately satisfied. Golden Rule Vitamins, Inc. is an international company, listed on the New York Stock Exchange. Why shouldn't they make me thin? Nobody believed in the telephone either. Wasn't the first steamship called Fulton's Folly?

Most Troubling Aspect of the Brochure: There's a picture of the company president and he looks like a male model, he looks like he spent an hour on his hair. Now if the pills worked, then why would he need to spend all that time on his hair?

Monday, March 9, 1987. (195 lbs.) Wilson told me that she has decided to study French on Tuesday and Thursday evenings. I've agreed to baby-sit. PBDE and O has a Paris office. If she were assigned to Paris, it would be a promotion.

NOEL: "What about us?"

WILSON: "You come too."

NOEL: "Mais je ne parle pas français."

WILSON: "Tant mieux!"

25

ARE YOU ASKING
ME TO LIE?

SUNDAY, MARCH 15, 1987. The Ides of March kid survives another year in almost perfect anonymity. They don't know at work. Thank the Lord for such blessings. We had a small, a family, celebration. Bart gave me a card with a picture of Horton on it. Wilson gave me a Swiss army knife with scissors.

"Oh, thanks," I said. "I've always wanted to be in the army. Particularly the Swiss army. Keeping the world safe for cuckoo clocks."

WILSON: "And Nazi gold."

NOEL: "I stand corrected. And Nazi gold."

WILSON: "It's for your toenails. I hate your toenails."

Monday, March 16, 1987. Got a call from Che. His rich, powerful father remarried two years ago. The doxie is younger than Che, and they've had a child young enough to be Che's. Young enough to be Che's grandchild, actually, if they lived in, let's see, backwoods West Virginia. Che's been doing a good deal of babysitting. "My father gives me time off from work to do it." We compared child-care techniques. I warned Che about popped balloons. I asked him if he hated the baby food manufacturers as much as I've grown to hate the baby food manufacturers. He did. I offered to send him a copy of the letter I sent to Gerber.

My ankle hurts always now. Except when I'm running. Which means my ankle hurts twenty-three hours a day. I left work early, came out to Bedford Hills, went to my doctor. He's an Englishman. Doctor Charles Codrington. Yes, he is descended from the admiral. Codrington looked at my ankle. He took an X ray. Then he looked at the X ray and made tisking sounds. Then he poked me twice in the belly. Then he told me I should lose weight. I told him I knew I should lose weight.

CODRINGTON: "Or else you shouldn't run so much."

I'm going to send away for that weight loss kit. Golden Rule Vitamins, Inc. Why ever not? Probably the pills won't make me fat. The pounds might even melt away. I won't always need to run. The pill program costs $100 a pop. On the other hand, I just spent $175 to have an X ray taken and my belly poked.

Monday, March 23, 1987. (197 lbs.) 4 P.M. When I come down hard on my right foot, pain shoots up to my hairline, my eyes cross. Running provides its own painkiller, so I was able to go five miles today alone. Tomorrow I'll walk instead.

Wednesday, March 25, 1987. (198 lbs.) I had long believed that if I ever stopped running, something bad would happen. And you know what? I was right.

Yesterday, I didn't run. I came into the street at 45th, went east until I hit 2nd Avenue, just as if I were aiming for the Y. My ankle's so sore, I started out limping. When I got going, things loosened up. I had my Walkman and was listening to *The Best of the Big Chill.* "I heard it through the grapevine."

Running, we go north, to get near the river. I didn't want my
pals to see me walking. So I went south. The sidewalks are relatively clear in that section of Gotham. You can work off steam
without catching an umbrella strut in the eye.

Then I saw a twosome up ahead. I thought I recognized the
woman's shoes. Plus she had auburn hair. To the waist. I couldn't
see her face. It was buried in his shoulder. He had his arm
around her. They made an attractive young couple. And very
much in love.

I put my head down, turned into a side street. Didn't want to
be rude. I got back here, called Wilson's office. I left a message
that she should phone me. Long hair isn't all that unusual.

3 P.M. I called again. I left another message.

Thursday, March 26, 1987. The nanny dropped Bart off in the
evening. So everything must be OK. I mean she wouldn't cheat
on me and then also use me when her nanny had a dentist
appointment.

I figured Wilson would pick Bart up. Bart and I made a sign.
"Marry Us," it said. We put it out the window of my apartment.
Clearly visible from the parking lot. Wilson didn't come pick the
boy up. It was the nanny again. Which made for an awkward
moment. My not wanting to marry the nanny. I'll call Wilson
tomorrow. "Be cool boy." Or else she'll phone me. Probably she'll
phone me.

Friday, March 27, 1987. In office. This is eating me alive. I'll call
now. I'll write about it as it's happening. Nothing bad ever happens, if I'm writing. Correction: Nothing at all ever happens if
I'm writing.

Now it's twenty minutes later. I called. Here's what happened. Exactly what happened. I was insistent. George, her secretary, said Wilson was busy. I said I'd hold. He said she'd probably be a while. I said it was an emergency and I'd hold for a while. So then she picked up.

WILSON: "How the hell are you?"

NOEL: "Fine. I guess."

WILSON "So what's the big emergency?"

NOEL: "No emergency, really."

WILSON: "OK. Good. Look, I have to get back to work."

NOEL: "There was one thing."

WILSON: "Shoot."

NOEL: "I was walking on 2nd Ave. At about 2 P.M. Couple of days ago."

WILSON (her voice had changed, although almost imperceptibly): "Why weren't you running? Don't you usually run in the middle of the day?"

NOEL: "My ankle is sore. I wanted to give it a break."

WILSON: "Oh, Noel, I am sorry. I know how you love to run."

NOEL: "Thanks." I waited for her to say something else. She didn't, so I blundered on. "This is going to sound ridiculous." I paused. She didn't say anything. "I thought I saw you."

WILSON: "Yes?"

NOEL: "With somebody."

She said "Yes" again, but her voice had changed, and this time I couldn't miss it.

NOEL: "You were. Well, you seemed to like him."

Then she came back on the line. Voice flat now. All business. "Listen, Noel, let me get this straight? Are you asking me to lie?"

In other and totally unrelated news, seven people were killed when a mail bomb went off at the corporate headquarters of Gerber Foods.

26

"I BELIEVE IN HEROES"

THURSDAY, JUNE 18, 1987. First the world news. The notorious Wordsworth Bomber killed a girl in Yonkers. She and her mother had been waiting on line at the Customer Service Desk at Crazy Eddie's. I know the place. Many's the happy hour I've whiled away on that same line. The girl was pretty. She turns out to have been a chess prodigy. Somebody—perhaps her mother—has produced a picture of the live girl getting a chess prize. The papers are all running this alongside the shot of her death. Great contrast. They couldn't have staged a more arresting display. In the second picture, the death picture, there's a Crazy Eddie sign: "You have to be Insane."

The bomber left a note. The opening couplet of Wordsworth's "Resolution and Independence": "There was a roaring in the wind all night; The rain came heavily and fell in floods."

The story's so big, they're giving almost no attention to the cyanide killer. Somebody is putting cyanide in the Excedrin. Two people have already died.

That's the end of the world news. Local news? I have an Excedrin headache.

Friday, June 19, 1987. (199 lbs.) I got my package from Golden
Rule Vitamins, Inc. I'm supposed to take seven pills a day in a
variety of colors.

July 2, 1987

President
ACME Hardware and Home Essentials
Chicago, Illinois

To Whom It May Concern:

I don't know if this is true for executives
at Acme Hardware, but I know it's true for me.
Just when I think life's gotten unbearable, it
surprises me. And gets worse.

I bought the Executive Weight Master at your
Jefferson Valley store. The scale I had owned
was difficult to read. Your scale seemed all
right. I still wasn't thin, but least I knew how
fat I was. Or thought I knew.

I run out of a YMCA. I knew the Y had a
doctor's scale (one of those big ones that will
also measure your height, and has little sliding
weights), but I'd never used it before today.
Today I ran eight miles with this guy named
Charlie, who always uses the doctor's scale. So
after the run, I too used the doctor's scale.
This morning, before the run, I weighed 196 on
the scale you sold me. This afternoon, before
lunch and after an eight-mile run, I weighed 207
pounds. You do the math.

I may be mistaken, but I have the distinct
impression that American corporations were once

more responsible, more serious about their
products and promises. My father was an Episcopalian minister, and fought the introduction of
the new Book of Common Prayer. When he was a boy
growing up outside of Boston, Massachusetts, he
bought a box of Cracker Jacks, in which he found
no prize. He fired off a letter to the president
of the Cracker Jacks company, and got back a
handwritten note, not from a public relations
officer, but from the actual president of the
company.

Sincerely,

Noel Hammersmith

July 4, 1987. Here's to the red-white-and constitutionally dishonest. It'll be like baby clothes, where only an abnormally small
child fits into the sizes as they are labeled. All one-year-olds are
wearing clothes for eighteen months, and all mothers can boast
about their child's robustness. If the same market forces are ever
brought to bear on the manufacture of bathroom scales, every
American will weigh 350 pounds but will have a bathroom scale
that says he weighs 138.

Then we're all going to need additional food and doubtless
this will be "fat free." Har, har. Next we will require more com-
modious and dishonestly labeled clothes. There will be regular
pants, and then easy-fit pants. The easy-fit pants will be the
same size, only for fatter people. Thousands will find employ-
ment in the construction of easy-fit coffins.

Monday. Blue Monday. August 10, 1987. (197 lbs.) On the
crooked scale. Still taking my pills. Unfortunately, they make

me feel odd, dizzy. The only way I know to clear my head is
to eat.

I hate feeling dizzy. I also hate wielding power. Under Tollah,
I didn't have to. But Layman likes to wield his power. So now he
wants me to wield mine as well. He has asked me to pass out
time sheets to my editors.

NOEL: "Just as if they were secretaries?"

LAYMAN: "Just as if they had real work to do."

I'm to pass the sheets out at start of business every morning and
pick them up at 5 P.M. But not before 5 P.M. Campbell is in the
habit of leaving before 5 P.M. And Campbell is not alone.

In other local news, little sister wants to leave Tony. She called
to tell me. "When I was single my pockets did jingle," she said.

"Did not," I said.

"You and I could double-date," she said.

"I'm too old to double-date."

"Are not."

"I was born too old to double-date."

"Well, it's either leave Tony, or murder him in his bath."

Monday, August 17, 1987. (198 lbs.) It's 9:30 A.M. I've passed out
the dreaded sign-in sheets and am back at the blue Selectric III.
Another lost weekend. I ran, vacuumed, waxed the floors. When I
was done, the place looked worse than ever. Read Che's manuscript. Where did he get that overblown style? I figure most art is
derivative, and so picked up a copy of *Soldier of Fortune*. Che is
nowhere on the masthead. Page 100-and-something, you can
order a bulletproof vest for $319 plus shipping and handling.
Page 100-and-something-else, you can buy a bulletproof vest for
$139 plus shipping and handling. I wonder if anybody buys the
cheap body armor. Maybe just to wear in the bedroom.

There are advertisements for action specials, single issues of
the magazine devoted to isolated deeds of heroism. "Female

Warrior Kills Commie Platoon," with a picture of a girl. Her hair's all done up, and her nails painted. She looks great, but not exactly rugged. If she walked through a sprinkler, it would take a half an hour to make repairs. She's sighting out at the reader with her M16.

I can imagine how the cadres might respond to this threat: "Heah, sweetpants. Shoot me next." I fear that none of this speaks too well for the credibility of my prime writer.

Thursday, August 20, 1987. (199 lbs.) This on my dishonest scale. I phoned my local Golden Rule distributor. She was wonderfully sweet. She said she admires me for running every day. "I wish I had the discipline." She said she'd lost 39 pounds. With no exercise. But not with plan C. "I don't have the willpower. I needed a stronger dose." So I ordered plan B. Costs? One hundred and ninety-five dollars. Now there's a poke in the belly for you.

President
Wegner Swiss Army Knife Registration
c/o Precise International
P.O. Box 5512
Orangeburg, NY 10962

Friday, August 28, 1987

To Whom It May Concern:

In March of this year I received one of your genuine Swiss army knives as a gift from a woman then very close to me. "It'll last a lifetime," I said, when I opened the package.

The scissors are already broken. The small band of metal used to make the blades pop apart

after you've cut something has snapped off.
Every other implement is fine, but then the
scissors are all I ever had any use for. I
suspect that if my knife broke, many other
knives will also break.

My father was an Episcopalian priest in
upstate New York. He fought the introduction of
the revised Book of Common Prayer. Thomas
Cranmer wrote the original, a book so holy he
was burned at the stake for his efforts.

When my father was a young man, and growing
up outside of Boston, he once bought a box of
Cracker Jacks in which there was no prize. He
wrote a letter to the president of the Cracker
Jacks company, and got back an apology in
return, a note so finely worded that it was
framed, and hung on the wall behind his desk
in the rectory. With the note the president of
the company--not a public relations officer, but
the president himself--had enclosed an entire
box of prizes, one of every prize they made.
The best of these was a tiny pair of metal
scissors so sharp that they actually cut
through paper.

Sincerely,
Noel Hammersmith

Thursday, September 10, 1987. The shower door broke again.
This time the super says I have to pay to have it repaired. "I don't
know what you've been doing in there," he said, as if I'd been
sponging off playmates, instead of simply hanging on in solitary
nudity, trying to keep my weight reasonable.

Friday, September 11, 1987. I went to the Y for a run at noon and
found Tom and Giff already back and in the shower. Why didn't
Giff call and tell me they were running early? I could have made
it. Also, they were whispering when I came in. I thought I heard
Giff say "The No Man." Who else could that be?

Meantime, at work, Fay's decided that the businesspeople
need to be profiled, too, in order to give "an accurate image of
our corporate culture." She's interviewing Layman. I passed
them in the hall recently. "But I'm an old-fashioned girl," I heard
her say. "I believe in heroes."

27

KILLED BY ROCKS

Fulton Basque Holloway
Holloway, Holloway & Stone
230 Benefit Street
Providence, Rhode Island 02903

September 12, 1987

Dearest Fulton:

I suspected that you and Kat weren't sleeping
in the same bedroom anymore. There was a certain
erect tone to your prose.

Have you considered counseling?

I've worked on a lot of self-help books in my
time. Most of them are nonsense. Bromides.
Designed to sell self-help books.

If I had to boil millions of pages of expert
advice down to the four things I've learned,
they would be:

1. Don't get fat!
2. Don't get sick!
3. Don't get poor!

   4. And don't get married! But if you do get
married, you're not supposed to get divorced.
Marriage, like MS, is a condition for which they
don't have a cure. There's such a thing as
remission, of course. Moderate exercise and low-
fat diet can slow advancing decrepitude.

Love, No

P.S. I have no reason to believe that Kat is
involved with another man. Months ago, when this
started, I tried to warn you both off. Please
try to remember that?

Monday, September 14, 1987. Hit 214 lbs. A house record. I
spoke again with the woman at the Golden Rule. Now I'm on
plan A. It cost $299 for a month plus tax. But this way I'll lose
weight while sleeping.

Her name is Marge Fallon, or did I already tell you that?
Marge said, "Some people have willpower. They can make plan B
work for them, or even plan C. I don't have willpower. It's better
to be honest with yourself. Like Nietzsche said: 'To thine own
self be true and thou shalt not be false to any other.'"

I was going to skip lunch. But Little Sister is in town, supposed to be visiting me. She's in town, but she's not visiting me.
She's got a whole new crop of gentleman callers. She was twenty
minutes late at Nanni's. Came up behind me and put her hands
over my eyes. "Guess who?"

"Messalina, the Countess DeWinter, Madame Defarge?"

When she was at Emma Willard, my sister used to dress like a
woman of means. Now that she's a woman of means, she dresses
like she's at Emma Willard. She had on white sneakers, black

jeans, and a man's blue shirt, unbuttoned so that you could see the top of her black lace brassiere. I tried to set down some rules.

NOEL: "Don't even mention your husband."

LITTLE SISTER: "I thought you liked Tony."

NOEL: "That's the point. I don't want to hear."

LITTLE SISTER: "But you're my brother."

NOEL: "What does that have to do with anything?"

LITTLE SISTER: "In sickness and in health."

NOEL: "What about my friendship?"

LITTLE SISTER: "Tony loves you."

NOEL: "He also trusts me."

LITTLE SISTER: "So? He's glad I went to the city. 'It'll cheer you up.' That's what he said. Besides which, I'm going to Hermes. I'm going to buy him a fabulous necktie."

NOEL: "Just what every man wants to be: a well-dressed cuckold."

Thursday, October 1, 1987. I called Marge Fallon at Golden Rule. I've spent more than $600 on their diet pills and gained weight. "I'm running out of money," I told her, which was a lie. But it got her attention.

"Weight loss we can't always guarantee," she said. "Metabolisms vary widely. But money we can guarantee. You could become a distributor. Sell these pills to other people. You must know of other people who want to lose weight. Start them on plan C. It's really quite reasonable."

So it isn't the weight loss business at all, they're in. It's the money loss business. They sell promises for cash. Just like us.

They're doing well. As are we. *The Pyramid Diet* book is selling like hula hoops. Like Cabbage Patch dolls. The plastic cube is a stroke of genius. People like to buy objects. That's the trouble with books. Once you've bought one book, you've bought them all. Unless you buy a pop-up book, there will be no tactile surprises. The form hasn't changed dramatically in hundreds of years. But if you give the customer something he can touch, he'll often go for the words as well. Remember the pet rock? It wasn't the rock they were buying, it was the instructions. Lesson: Most people would rather buy a rock than a book. They think rocks are real and ideas are not real. But many more people have been killed by ideas than have been killed by rocks.

28

SKIP DESSERT

I HAD AMELIA connect me with the Westchester County Office of Consumer Affairs. I got a consumer advocate who seemed to have just woken up. I asked if she'd seen the ads Golden Rule Vitamins, Inc. has been running. "All over the place?"

The consumer advocate wanted to know which ads.

"The ones where they promise that you'll lose weight while earning thousands of dollars a month in the privacy of your own home. 'You have nothing to lose but your shame.'"

The consumer advocate thought she had seen the ads. "Probably I saw them," she said.

"Well, I spent more than $600 on diet pills. I took plans C, B, and finally A. Plan A is the one where you also lose weight while sleeping. The advertisement guaranteed that the pounds would melt away."

"And they didn't melt away?" she asked.

"Nope," I said. "I actually got fatter."

"Oh, dear!" she said.

"Isn't this fraud?" I asked.

The consumer advocate wouldn't say. "I'm not a lawyer," she said. "I wouldn't want to throw around a word like 'fraud.'"

"So what should I do?" I asked.

"Maybe you should eat less." That's what she said. I need a consumer advocate to tell me to skip dessert?

29

A TRAITOR TO MY SEX

THURSDAY, OCTOBER 15, 1987. (217 lbs.) Another house record. Another bomb went off on Madison Avenue today. Campbell and Nancy went out to look at it. I asked them what they saw. "A lot of blue sawhorses. Cops. A traffic jam."

Monday, October 19, 1987. The bomber isn't the number one story today. The bomber is the number two story. The number one story is the plunging Dow. The Dow Jones Industrials dropped more than 200 points this morning. It rebounded forty points, but nobody was seeing this rebound as a trend.

Found a good quote in yesterday's reading: Life is an effort that deserves a better cause.

Tuesday, October 20, 1987. I called Jeff Bigg. He said we should get out now. I said "How bad is it?" He said, "I'll try and pick up the pieces." On Monday, when the market was plummeting—it fell 508 points in one day—George Peabody (aka Pig) ran with me and he was smiling. I thought that if anybody was going to

153

get killed off, it would be the Pig. I figured a bear market would clean his clock. I was mistaken. He's a wily old pig.

Only the stupid and self-satisfied survive.

The crash has wiped out more than $500 billion in stock equity. Since August 25, the market has dropped 1,000 points, 36 percent, which is nearly three times what it dropped in 1929. At Shearson Lehman Brothers, they tacked up a sign: "To the lifeboats!"

Which lifeboats?

―――――――――――

Wednesday, October 21, 1987. The business has been sold. The best little publishing house in the world will henceforth be owned by Pretty Kitty. No, I'm not kidding. We were bought by an international conglomerate that sells cat food and cat toiletries. Get that? Cat toiletries. And us, the guys who brought Kafka to America.

Called Jeff Bigg with two g's. He said, "It's over for you kid. You're out of the market."

NOEL: "And what was the damage?"

JEFF BIGG: "You like your work right?"

NOEL: "Not particularly."

JEFF BIGG: "Well, you can't retire."

―――――――――――

Friday, October 23, 1987. (219 lbs.) Layman phoned. He'd been looking at our schedule. Wanted to know what was happening in the literary world.

NOEL: "Joseph Brodksy won the Nobel Prize for Literature."

LAYMAN: "Brodkey?"

NOEL: "No, Brodsky. For his all-embracing authorship, imbued clarity of thought, and poetic intensity."

LAYMAN: "I never heard of him."

NOEL: "He's Russian. He was in a Chinese restaurant in London when they brought him the news. He was with John Le Carre. Name's actually David Cornwall. You read Le Carre?"

LAYMAN: "No."

NOEL: "Anyway. Brodsky said, 'It's a big step for me and a small one for mankind.'"

Nothing from Layman.

NOEL: "That's funny. You're supposed to laugh."

LAYMAN: "How much does he get?"

NOEL: "Three hundred and forty thousand dollars."

LAYMAN: "He makes the people who gave him the prize look stupid."

NOEL: "Oh."

LAYMAN: "So the one book you've got in the pipeline that has any real promise is something you've been sitting on for years. Your bomb book. Why won't you finish that?"

NOEL: "The writer has to finish it. The writer's a nut."

LAYMAN: "And Joseph Brodsky isn't a nut?"

NOEL: "Brodsky can write. Which is most of what you want in a writer."

LAYMAN: "Is it really?"

NOEL: "Yes."

LAYMAN: "What have we offered this guy? By way of advance?"

NOEL: "Twenty-five thousand."

LAYMAN: "Double it, if he can get the book in within the year. No, triple it with the first payment on acceptance of a workable draft."

So I called Che, who seemed almost to expect the heightened interest. Which is odd. Since I'm his editor. And I was surprised.

Monday, November 9, 1987. (220 lbs.) I read the paper before I started on my growing pile of manuscripts, which I should not have done. What did I learn? I learned that any real advance on the genetic origins of cancer is years away. I learned that the Know-Nothings are making a lot of noise about the stock market crash. They hint darkly about an international Jewish banking conspiracy. They say it's time for "the people" to take back the land of our fathers. They say we aren't reproducing enough to keep our population level. They say that at the same time, we're swamped with immigrants. We're getting 800,000 legal immigrants a year and another 300,000 illegal ones. They want to pass a law to keep Jews from handling money. They want also to close the border.

What else did I learn? That I must eat breakfast. People who eat breakfast weigh less and live longer.

Tuesday, November 10, 1987. A white crested cockatoo kept in the front lobby was badly hurt and had to be destroyed, but no people were injured yesterday when a bomb went off in Orangeburg at the New York offices of Precise International. They manufacture the Swiss army knife. Too bad about the bird.

Wednesday, November 18, 1987. 10 A.M. Surprise! surprise! The people at Pretty Kitty think we're overextended. Well, hit me with a fish. They think they paid too much for a trade publishing house. However small and choice.

Layman came in this morning. You know, he's lost weight. I wonder if it's the pyramid diet. He likes a prop. He'd carry a cane, or a riding crop, if he could think of it. He had a folder. In the folder he had the sales figures on *The Pyramid Diet*. He must be studying his self-help books, because he pulled this weird, unsettling maneuver. He asked me a question about one of the manuscripts piled on my sofa, and I had to get up and look at the pages in question in order to answer it. Then, when I was up, he sat at my desk. So I had to sit in the visitor's chair.

LAYMAN: "Did you know we had one big success this year? Count them. One. *The Pyramid Diet.*"

NOEL: "I know that."

LAYMAN: "Which leaves me with one burning question."

NOEL: "Shoot."

LAYMAN: "You've had successes in the past, many successes. Fay Waterman has never had a success before. She doesn't even work in editorial. Was the purchase of *The Pyramid Diet* your idea, or hers?"

NOEL: "It was hers."

LAYMAN: "Hers entirely?"

NOEL: "Yup."

Thursday, November 19, 1987. Tony phoned last night. Furious. At me. And my "bitch-cunt sister." But mostly at me. "You knew all along that she was cheating?"

NOEL: "No, Tony, I didn't know."

TONY: "You're an asshole, Noel. A lying asshole. A traitor to your sex."

30

THE JAVA
IS A SACRAMENT

MONDAY, DECEMBER 14, 1987. (223 lbs.) "Imprisoned in every fat man, a thin one is wildly signaling to be let out." So wrote Cyril Vernon Connolly. I signal wildly. Nobody comes. Nobody cares.

Fat and sad as I am, I still adore Grand Central this time of year, the dark bustle, the smells of coffee, perfume and wet wool. They've gussied the old place up with shops and advertising. And haven't cleaned the ceiling in years. But still it's grand. A delight for the eye. I admire the marble, I relish the polished brass.

I've been told that you could fit a seven-story building into the main concourse. The space is impressive, but so is the crowd. We're a horde, a cast of thousands. In the winter we actually look like an army, like characters out of those grainy newsreels of the Russian Revolution, a gathering of long coats, hats, and heavy boots. We have taken the Winter Palace. The marble floor is streaked with melted snow. The grandest and most elaborate buildings in this great Empire have fallen to the people. I have seen the future, and it works. From nine to five, it works.

Last week they put up bleachers in front of the wall that faces the grand staircase across the terminal. Today there was a choir there, girls standing on the seats, belting out carols.

They've dusted off the knife displays in the window of Hof-
fritz. Zaro's is all tarted up with ribbons and bows. The Java is a
sacrament.

31

TUESDAY, DECEMBER 15, 1987. 4 P.M. (224 lbs.) Somebody must've bought a brand new purple marker, because the railroad platform was dramatically touched up this morning. The actresses in the movie posters all had moustaches. The actors had daggers jutting from their chests, with great comic drops of blood falling away. There are three newspaper dispensers. The one that sells *The New York Post* had "LIES!" written on it. The one that sells *USA Today* had "LIES WITH PICTURES!!" scrawled across its plastic window. No real argument from this reader. But I was shocked when I walked far enough down the platform to see the machine for *The New York Times*. "MORE LIES!!!" our prophet had written. "THE WORST ONES." And then on the coin box he had printed "OUT OF ORDER." The machine was not out of order, and so our revolutionary was a liar himself. And yet I couldn't shake the conviction that he had a point.

My father, of course, had the churchman's horror of disfigurements however petty. Any eyesore was taken as a personal insult. The parish used to spend a Saturday every spring and one every fall cleaning up at the public park, and out at the mouths of the limestone caves, where the teenagers used to like to picnic. Dover Plains is famous for its caves. He wanted always to return the countryside to some Wordsworthian splendor.

160

There was a time when Meadow, grove, and stream,
The earth and every common sight,
To me did seem
Apparelled in celestial light,

He loved Wordsworth. "The World is too much with us late and soon," he'd say, coming down to breakfast on a winter morning. "Getting and spending we lay waste our powers."

Close my eyes, and I can see him at the pulpit, standing straight as a soldier at attention: Rejoice! Rejoice!

I wish I had that sort of faith. I don't believe in my own writers. Speaking of which, Che dropped by yesterday, about fifteen minutes before I planned to go out for my run. He's hiding it, but I can tell he's pleased about the enlargement of his advance. Also, he likes my new, big office. He sat right down in my guest chair.

Che's the sort who's going to have his Nobel acceptance speech fine-tuned before he's completed his first manuscript. He's been thinking a lot about his peers. He wanted to know if I knew that Orwell didn't write anything until he was thirty. He wanted to know if I knew that Ann Beattie used sometimes to wear her boyfriend's clothes.

NOEL: "Yes. And yes."

CHE: "And are you acquainted with any writers? I mean any famous ones?"

NOEL: "Dr. Martin Roan."

CHE: "The diet doctor?"

NOEL: "He had a couple of best-sellers."

CHE: "I mean writers. Creative people. Artists: Saul Bellow, Ernest Hemingway, Jean Auel?"

NOEL: "No."

All this interest in the literary world hasn't exactly improved his prose. The book falls into two sections: the screed and the drama.

The screed is a longish essay about the nation being "on the brink," to coin a phrase, and him being a patriot. Something along the lines of Patrick Henry. "Is life so dear, or peace so sweet . . ." The drama is a heavily clichéd scene of a Christmas Eve bombing in Grand Central Terminal. His style owes more to movies than to life or even books. All the women are beautiful, the men purposeful, the children innocent. There's a lot of panning in on the wastebin with the explosives in it ticking ominously.

This morning I could see that he was warming up to tell me badly again the story which he had already written badly.

CHE: "What's the first real sign that something is about to go wrong?"

NOEL: "I don't know. The birds stop singing, even the insects."

CHE: "This isn't a western. I'm talking urban."

NOEL: "The police then?"

CHE: "Buzz, wrong again. The first real tip-off will be the arrival of a TV crew."

32

THEY AREN'T SHIITES

I PHONED CHE at home yesterday evening, tried to encourage him to actually write something about the terrorists, name names. "I know you have a feeling that the world's going to hell in a handbasket. To some extent we share that feeling, but it's not enough to base a book on. We need to know who these people are."

The next morning, another bomb went off. The blast was in Stamford, at the regional headquarters of Pretty Kitty Inc. They found a piece of a Wordsworth poem:

> *Our birth is but a sleep and a forgetting;*
> *The Soul that rises with us our life's Star,*
> *Hath had elsewhere its setting,*
> *And cometh from afar;*
> *Not in entire forgetfulness,*
> *And not in utter nakedness,*
> *But trailing clouds of glory do we come*
> *From God, who is our home.*

I do feel like an old man these days. And certainly forgetful. Giff won't run with me anymore. "Too damn slow."

Friday, December 18, 1987. 6 P.M. The bad manuscripts pile up. Amelia leaves a pink phone message on my desk whenever anybody calls. I come back from my run and it looks like it's been snowing in here, large, pink flakes. From writers, other editors, even the people in production. A.S.A.P. That's what they all say. "A.S.A.P."

I got an envelope from Tony's office. No letter. But then I never got letters when he liked me either. Enclosed was a story about Ginny, and her partner. This was a page from *Time*. Half the page was devoted to a reproduction of "The Marriage of John Hinckley to Jodie Foster." Somebody has bought it for $50,000. This is the painting that used to block the way to the broom closet. I hated it then. I hate it now.

Roan called. I'm so rattled that when Amelia told me he was on the line, I let her put him through. Stupid! He was furious about the way Fay had cut his manuscript. He thinks I did it. "If you were a doctor, all your patients would die."

No, I didn't tell him it was Fay. I might not have made her exact cuts. But it was a fat book. Plus, how to explain I'd given his manuscript to somebody in public relations. I went to the bathroom. I took the last stall, and sat.

The seat moved. I don't know why, but this freaked me. The one place you're supposed to feel safe and they hadn't bothered to use enough glue, or else to get the pipes right, and so the ceramic bowl wasn't stuck to the floor. Nothing broke, but as I sat, the whole unit settled.

God is in the details. Excellence is in the last 3 percent of effort. And whoever installed this toilet obviously didn't believe in God, or in the possibility of true excellence here on earth. And If I know anything about contemporary thought, he didn't believe it existed anywhere else either.

Dostoyevsky is supposed to have said that the true measure of a society is in its prison. What about the toilets? What if we can't even be bothered to construct for ourselves a comfortable place to shit?

In Manhattan you have to own an apartment, join a club, or buy a meal in order to take a piss indoors. And taking a piss outdoors, say against a tree, why that's illegal.

We all talk a great game, we hum the advertising jingles, parrot the cheery speeches of corrupt politicians, but what do we really believe? We really believe we're running out of time. We really believe that if there isn't an about-face soon, we're going to leave this planet in a smoking ruin.

We're in a race with the machines, and the machines are winning. We're enslaved by our own creations.

Prophets have seen it coming. "Man has mounted science and is now run away with," Henry Adams wrote about the *Monitor* and the *Merrimack*. "I firmly believe that before many centuries more, science will be the master of man. The engines he will have invented will be beyond his strength to control. Some day science will have the existence of mankind in its power, and the human race shall commit suicide by blowing up the world."

Which is why all these little failings strike at my heart. We're cutting ourselves out of the picture. Houses are made of sheetrock and sticks instead of plaster and stone. Chairs and toilets are uncomfortable. Everything breaks. We're setting the stage, making annihilation appropriate and therefore inevitable. We're the ghosts in the machine.

I don't think of this often. Not consciously. And yet it's there, always, the prospects of extinction, like an incipient sinus headache.

Is that why I'm sad? Or is it the problem of having to teach Che to write? Came back from my run and he was in my office.

The phone rang; I grabbed it.

It was Fay. She has a friend somewhere out there with connections and has been told that *The Pyramid Diet* is number one on the *Publishers Weekly* hardcover best-seller list.

FAY: "I don't believe we've ever had a number one best-seller before. Not in hardcover." I tried to keep her on the phone but couldn't. Obviously she had other calls to make. Che came over to the front of my desk. His mood had changed.

CHE: "You don't believe that this is going to happen?"

NOEL: "You mean the book, or the terrorists' bombings?"

CHE: "The bombings are already happening."

NOEL: "We have no evidence that they are connected with the terrorists you talk about."

CHE: "They're connected."

NOEL: "Prove it then."

CHE (giving his back to Noel, staring out the window): "Is that Saint Patrick's?"

NOEL: "Yes, but you were saying?"

CHE: "I was saying that you don't believe in me."

NOEL: "I've heard that one before."

CHE: "I bet you have. In any case, you don't believe this book is going to happen."

NOEL: "That's up to you."

CHE: "Is it?"

NOEL: "Absolutely."

Che left the window, came around behind my desk. I wish he wouldn't do that. It's a flanking movement that a lot of people try nowadays. I believe it was in Michael Korda's book *Success*. Che's breath smelled of peppermint Life Savers. "If I were from Harvard, or the University of Pennsylvania. If I had clippings, then you'd want this book, no matter how badly written. You think that because I've made a mess of my own life that means I don't know what's going on in the world."

NOEL: "What are you talking about. First you have to write the book."

CHE: "Why don't you write it for me. Or patch it together from what you've got."

NOEL: "What?"

CHE: "You do that for celebrities. Sometimes you even do it for academics."

NOEL: "Rarely. Plus you aren't a celebrity. Or an academic, really. Certainly this project would be more attractive if you had some professional or academic credentials. Or even if you had written up your theory for the op-ed page of *The New York Times*.

CHE: "I've written for the *Times*. A half a dozen pieces."

NOEL: "How come you never told me this before?"

Che turned, walked to the door, and stopped. "They didn't run the pieces I wrote for the op-ed page. I wasn't accepted. Nor was I surprised."

NOEL: "And why is that?"

CHE: "Because they don't like me."

NOEL: "Because who doesn't like you?"

CHE: "The people who control the newspaper."

NOEL: "And who controls the newspaper?"

CHE: "Don't pretend you don't know who controls *The New York Times*."

NOEL (almost bored now): "No, Che, I don't know. Who controls *The New York Times*?

CHE: "Well, they aren't Shiites."

33

CATCHING UP

ON MY READING

TUESDAY, DECEMBER 22, 1987. (225 lbs.) In office 3 P.M. 'Tis the season, all right. There's a story in the paper today about a nursing student from New Rochelle who put her newborn son into a dumpster and then went to a local dance hall. Even *The New York Times* ran it on the front page, right next to the Wordsworth Bomber update. The Wordsworth Bomber is in the paper every day. Like the weather. Only more important.

Oops! I ran into Layman in the hall, yesterday on the way out, and he gave me a big grin. "Good evening, good man," he said.

"Good evening, asshole," I said. I don't know why I said it. This was not smart. But then I didn't know it was coming. You can't guard against an action, when it hasn't even passed through your mind. Must have been the "good morning, good man," that set me off. I knew Layman to be a shit, but didn't think him capable of such sophisticated and mannerly hypocrisy.

Same day. At home. I brought a manuscript to read on the train. Do you know that the trains out of New York were just about as fast in 1887 as they are today? Plus, in Grand Central, the lights keep going out. You'd think they'd send a couple of men down there to clean off the contacts. But no. That would be too much trouble.

Wednesday, December 23, 1987. Late. Later than I think. I got in a full hour late today. The train broke down outside of Yonkers. Of course it was the one day I hadn't brought anything to read. So I just sat there and looked at my hands. Plus I missed my morning meeting with Fay. She said she'd be back in the afternoon. She didn't show up until 7:30 P.M. I was dozing over a manuscript and thought maybe she'd forgotten, when I heard the knock on the door, rose and answered it. Fay's lipstick seems to have gotten darker with her corporate advance. First she sat in one of the guest chairs, looked at her shoes for a bit before breaking the silence.

FAY: "I said I wanted to be the one to talk with you."

NOEL: "Thanks."

She nodded, came over, and sat on the edge of my desk. This is what Layman used to do before he learned the trick of actually sitting in your own chair. She's picked up his mannerisms along with his marketing skills. And his sensitivity.

FAY: "They say you can't follow through on the simplest orders."

NOEL: "Like what?"

FAY (gesturing at the couch): "How many manuscripts have you got there unread?"

NOEL: "Some. I'll get to them."

FAY: "When?"

NOEL: "When I fucking well please."

FAY (turning to look me in the face): "I don't know how you got so bitter, so soon."

I shrugged.

FAY: "No, honestly, Andrew likes you. He's always talking to me about you. He admires your erudition."

NOEL: "All right, all right, Andrew Layman is a swell guy. A man of discernment and taste."

FAY: "I mean it. You've got to control yourself. I'm being a friend to you now."

NOEL (looking down at his desk. He could see a pencil. He could see the flare of her skirt. If he looked up, he would see her narrow waist): "Okay. You're right."

FAY: "Please don't be so childish."

NOEL: "I'm not. I was kidding. In real life I'm perfectly civil to Andrew Layman. Always have been."

Fay put a small hand on my shoulder, smiled awkwardly. "That's not what I hear. And right now you've got to be on your very best behavior. I want to work with you on this."

NOEL: "Okay. That would be fine. I'd like to work with you." I creaked back in my chair. "So what's happening?"

FAY: "We're hiring a new associate editor."

NOEL: "That's good. We need the manpower."

Fay (smiled weakly): "There's also the problem of space."

NOEL: "I hadn't thought of that."

FAY: "Here's the tentative plan. As approved by Layman. The new editor will move into my office."

NOEL: "Good, good."

Fay slipped forward off the desk, walked to the door, stood there, looking down at her hands. Said nothing.

NOEL: "So where will you go?"

FAY: "That's not for sure yet."

NOEL: "Tentatively. Where will you be going tentatively?"

FAY (looking at her hands with real interest now): "Tentatively Layman thinks I should move in here. In fact he insists. 'You had the biggest book,' he said. 'You should have the biggest office.' But of course the details need to be worked out."

NOEL: "Of course they do. And carefully. God is in the details."

She wants me to take the next day off, in order to avoid a "silly confrontation with Layman." She asked me to come in for an evening meeting with her alone. "At like 6 P.M. We can go over these manuscripts together, deal with them one way or another. Then I'll take you out to a stuffing dinner."

Fay started to leave, then came back and gave me a peck on the cheek. "Don't worry baby," she said. "We'll be sure to find you a place to sit."

In other and totally unrelated news, a passenger ferry crashed into an oil tanker south of Manila in the Philippines Sunday night. Both ships went down. They estimate that 1,500 people are dead.

Amelia stayed late. Layman had asked her to. People in Mr. Hammer-smith's position often steal company property, he had explained. Amelia reports that Noel waited an hour, until he was sure Fay had left the build-ing. Then he packed up the something like thirty manuscripts in three shopping bags and lugged them out to the elevator. Amelia says she went out to stop him. "What have you got there?" she asked. "None of your business," he said, and she went back into her office to phone Layman at home. "What's he got?" Layman asked. "Manuscripts," Amelia told him. "Let him go," Layman said.

When Noel reached his apartment building, he must have gone directly to the incinerator and started to feed the unread books into the fire. He had about half of them disposed of when 4C showed up.

"I must have shocked her, with my hair all ruffled, my suit wrinkled, and this great heap of manuscripts, one of which I was forcing through the metal door," he told us later. "She gave me a questioning look."

"Bonfire of the vanities?" she asked.

"No," Noel reported saying. " 'And I produced my last, best smile.' Just catching up on my reading."

34

OUR HERO, HE SAID

Editor's note: The conclusion of the book veers dangerously close to Noel's own improbable explanation. We went to whatever other sources we could discover, grilled them closely, but ultimately were forced to rely largely on Noel's words. Suffice it to say that Tom Janus adamantly denies the role Noel has given him. "Do you really suppose the NYPD would countenance a deception on this scale?" he said. So here, with a large grain of salt, is the story that we heard told.]

Christmas Eve afternoon and the sky above the Bedford Hills railroad station was iron gray. Snow had been promised, but when the Express to Manhattan wheezed to a stop at 4:08 P.M. it had not yet begun to fall. Noel boarded the rattler. He was to meet Fay at 6 P.M. In her office, his old office, THE OFFICE, the badminton court. He found a seat and unfolded the newspaper. The conductor who checked his ticket appeared to be quite drunk, but otherwise there was nothing to signal the momentary arrival of the great chill blowout of the Christian year. "Getting and spending we lay waste our powers."

Giff knew Noel was coming to town and had asked his friend to get in early enough to help pick out a present for the long-suffering wife, Lily. "My own personal martyr to love," he called her.

Giff had said, "I'm having a little on the side. I need your touch. I need the sort of bauble that would ordinarily be given by a man who is terrified of women. That way she'll think I'm terrified of women."

Noel had wanted to know how much time to allow.

GIFF: "Ten minutes. Twenty max."

NOEL: "It'll take that long just to get to Tiffany."

GIFF: "That's the advantage of shopping at Orvis. Orvis is two minutes from the terminal."

NOEL: "What are you planning to buy Lily at Orvis, then? A dog bed?"

GIFF: "A fly rod."

NOEL: "It's not my advice you need, it's a brain transplant. Actually I'm not sure the brain is involved."

GIFF: "Well, well the Noman's in a sour mood for the holiday. Somebody putting vinegar in your milk? Coal in your stocking?"

"None of your business," said Noel. They agreed to meet at 5 P.M. in the main concourse and at the bottom of the escalators that go up into the Pan Am Building.

By 5:02 P.M., Noel was just where he was supposed to be. No Giff. Noel waited ten minutes, then crossed the concourse and peered at the tape recorders and watches in the window of Terminal Cameras.

He kept looking back at the escalators. Still no Giff. They had a ten-minute rule for running dates. If the second runner didn't show up within ten minutes, the first runner went on ahead. At 5:22 P.M. having waited double the allotted time, Noel went out onto Lexington Avenue. There was no snow, although a gray-black sky was coming down, rather as if it were being lowered on ropes. Noel headed uptown for a few yards and then ducked into Grand Central Cameras. During the late 1980s, this store featured a video camera on a tripod in one of the outside windows. Shoppers who approached the display could see themselves on several TV screens, which were also in the window. Noel said he had found that his first glimpse of himself was always a shock, because he'd been made smaller and was presented at an angle quite unlike that which he'd grown to expect from a mirror. Once over this jolt, the sensation was not an unpleasant one. When in the neighborhood, he often paused in front of the camera.

On this particular Christmas Eve, a young Korean man with a handkerchief in the breast pocket of his neatly pressed suit had set himself up in front of the Handycam. He was wearing a suit and seemed to be making a speech. He didn't have a script, but was talking in the slow, even tones of a person who has memorized his material. "As leaders in the international time management industry," he said, "we are the products of our products."

Noel waited until it was clear that this performance was going to go on for some time, then he went back down the sidewalk. A squat little man with bad teeth and dressed in a gray cardigan sweater was selling flowers off a folding table that had been set outside the glass doors to the terminal. Noel bought three flowers that looked like roses. These were wrapped in a cone of brightly colored paper.

"Roses?" he asked.

"Fifteen dollars," said the old man, which wasn't exactly an answer.

With twenty more minutes to kill, Noel wandered south on Lexington, took a right at the corner, and headed up 42nd Street. He walked west past the Grand Hyatt, paused to look down into the window of Barnes and Noble. There was nothing in the display that he wanted to read: celebrity biographies, written by people who hardly knew the celebrities, about celebrities who hardly knew themselves. He also spotted the familiar carton that held *The All-Poison Diet,* and in the corner three of his alphabet books in paper. Noel reentered the terminal at the doors under the Park Avenue overpass and started down the long, gradual slope into the main concourse. It was here, in the huge chandeliered chamber to the left that the seven-year-old child he remembered had once waited for the train to sleep-away camp. Camp Beaver Pond: "I'm a beaver, you're a beaver, we are beavers all, and when we see a beaver, we give the beaver call."

Common knowledge has it that the first-ever sleep away is dreaded in anticipation, but relished in fact. Not for Noel. Camp Beaver Pond had been worse than anticipated. Much worse than anticipated. He was fat. The other boys didn't like him. He wet his sleeping bag.

The memory of how he had felt that afternoon after having been dropped off at the station came to him now with the force of revelation: a pale chubby boy alone, searching the faces of the other campers. Who is kind? Who is cruel? Who might be desperate enough to form an alliance with a child this sad? Between his knees, the boy had held a cheap canvas duffel, crammed with new and unfamiliar clothes, each item labeled in indelible Magic Marker: Noel Hammersmith, a name so dignified that it made a mockery of its owner. The dark wooden benches—gone now—had smelled of wax, the same wax used on the pews in his father's church.

Looking up and into the present, Noel caught sight of a tall, awkward, and vaguely familiar figure in the distance. The man ducked behind the brass information booth that stood in the middle of the concourse. It might easily have been a stranger. God knows there are other ponytails in the city, although mostly they don't skulk. Most of the time the Manhattan ponytail will strut. When Hammersmith reached the booth, the Che look-alike was gone.

Bleachers had been thrown up where the Kodak photo had used to be. And in front of the place where the illuminated photo had stood was a scene that might have been a Kodak moment. Life imitating art, imitating life. Young women in maroon jumpers and cream-colored turtlenecks were standing on the seats of the bleachers singing carols. There was a banner made of terry cloth with "West River High Heavenly Choir" printed on it in white block letters.

"Jin-gle bells, jin-gle bells, jin-gle all the way! Oh what fun it is to ride in a one horse o-pen sleigh! Hey!"

By now it was 5:45 P.M. It takes only a few minutes to get from the main concourse to the 37th floor of the Pan Am Building. Noel didn't want to be early. He'd once seen Fay drinking diet orange soda. He decided he would walk to Zaro's and pick up one Diet Coke and one Sunkist Diet Orange, two straws, and a handful of napkins. This would kill time. Also, when he met Fay they would have supplies. They could have the first part of the conversation in the big office, his office, her office, in No Man's land, before deciding to go out to a restaurant that Noel felt he could no longer comfortably afford.

Zaro's was all tarted up and stinking of gingerbread. The glass booths were topped with houses made of cake and draped with garlands of ever-green. The "specials" blackboard had "A Merry Merry Christmas from the staff at Zaro's" printed on it in red, white, and green chalk. Noel went to the end of the line.

The scene at the deli was beginning to take on an eerie familiarity. Christmas carols are evocative, of course, but Noel didn't think that was it. Was this a scene from a movie? A book? Che's book? That's right, Che's book. Guevara was always juxtaposing holiday scenes with tragedy. He had written up a bombing scene in Grand Central that read a lot like the diorama through which Noel was walking now. The man directly in front of Noel in line had a jacket with "Property of CBS Evening News" printed across the back.

What had Che said? It was a question. "What is the first sign that something is going wrong?"

"Police?"

"Buzz! Wrong again. The arrival of the TV crew."

"Yes, I know," Noel had said. "When they thrust a microphone into your face, it probably doesn't mean you won the lottery." Noel tapped the back of the man in front of him. "You work in TV?"

The stranger smiled shyly. "No," he said. "My brother-in-law used to."

So that was okay.

The carolers were now dreaming noisily of a white Christmas. The line was not moving. Noel looked at his watch. He was late.

He was about halfway to the escalator when he passed a young woman heading toward Zaro's. He caught a whiff of cheap perfume. The woman had an infant girl in a navy-blue MacClaren stroller and was holding the hand of a small boy in a green sweater with snowflakes. Noel did a double take. No, the boy was not Bart, of course, didn't remotely resemble the child he'd lost. The sweater was what Noel had recognized. Bart had had the same sweater. The infant girl in the stroller was crying. The boy was saying he wanted a "Cocola."

Noel stopped at the foot of the escalators and watched idly as the little party advanced toward Zaro's.

"You can't have Coke," the woman said. "A Coke will keep you up all night."

"But, Mommy, I'm thirsty," the boy said. "I need Cocola."

"Nobody needs Cocola," the woman said. The young mother was wearing black nail polish, black jeans, and a green flannel shirt with a white turtleneck underneath. The pocketbook matched the nail polish. The jeans were long and had been turned up at the cuffs, so that Noel could see the lining that matched the flannel of the shirt. She had on heels, stiletto heels. A sky blue nylon diaper bag had been attached to one of the handles of the stroller. She locked the stroller wheels, unhooked the diaper bag and put it on the top of the wastebin. The covers on the bins in Grand Central are built to slope. Objects could be balanced there, but only if carefully placed. *If there is a bomb,* Noel thought idly, *it'll be curtains for that diaper bag.*

The chorus had started in on a new song:

"Good King Wen-ces-las looked out On the Feast of Steph-en,

When the snow lay round a-bout, Deep and crisp and e-ven."

Fay was upstairs in the corner office. Fay was waiting. Probably there isn't a bomb, Noel thought. He just had bombs in his head. He'd been reading a lot about bombs in the papers. He'd seen explosives detonated often on TV and in movies. This sort of thing happened in movies and on TV. Never in life. This is life, thought Noel. I can tell because I'm still fat and my ankle hurts.

And yet he drifted away from the escalators. He began to walk hesitantly back toward Zaro's. He hadn't been genuinely alarmed, but now, with each step he took, the conviction grew that he was moving toward real danger. His heart pumped faster, his ears began to buzz. He stopped near the wastebin, stood in front of the young mother. Up close, she was quite pretty, with a pimple on her chin. Her nails were long and painted black. What had Giff said about black fingernail polish?

"Hello," Noel said. "I'm sure this is silly, but I'd like it if you got away from here."

"What?"

"This particular spot may be dangerous."

The woman smiled. "Of course it's dangerous," she said. "It's New York City."

"No," said Noel. "I mean right here. This place in particular. Just an intuition," he said, protecting his special knowledge.

"Thanks," she said, "but I'm tired. And Nicholas needs a drink."

"Oh, that's all right," said Noel. "If we just got away from here, I'd be happy to buy the boy a drink. I'd buy you a drink as well," he said, only realizing when he was done how lame that particular offer sounded.

Now the woman bristled. "Why ever should you buy me a drink?"

"I don't know," said Noel, shrugging helplessly. "It *is* Christmas Eve."

"That's all right," she said. "I've got a can of apple juice in here some-where." She smiled weakly, while she fished blindly in the diaper bag. "I believe I've even got a straw."

"Well then," Noel said, "could you do me a favor and get away from the wastebin?"

Now the woman was beginning to be annoyed. "Why?"

"I don't know," said Noel. "Germs?" he asked, almost plaintively.

"We'll take our chances," the young woman said.

Noel scratched himself nervously behind the left ear. "I'm going to be perfectly candid with you," he said. "This garbage bin may be dangerous. Very dangerous."

Now the woman looked alarmed. "I'm going to be perfectly candid right back," she said. "I don't think it was right to close all those state mental hospitals like they did, and put everybody out onto the street."

"Oh, come on," said Noel, who had tucked the flowers under one arm so that he could put both hands forward, the palms cupped upward, in a gesture of supplication. (See *Privacy Zone: Gestures, Distances, and What They Mean,* Acropolis Books, 1983.) "You know I'm not a nut." Then he smiled in a way he hoped might charm her. "Ask me anything. What day it is. The capital of Minnesota."

"All right, then, what's the capital of Minnesota?"

Noel shrugged. "Minnesota City?"

"Nope," said the woman. "You lose. Now leave us alone."

"All right," said Noel, rubbing his hands together. "We may be running out of time. It's really the boy I'm most worried about, but I'd sure feel a whole lot better about everything if you got away from this immediate area. How much trouble could that be?"

The woman was still searching in the sky blue diaper bag, refusing now to even make eye contact. "I promise I'll move on as soon as I'm done finding Nicholas something to drink."

Calmly really, when one considers how agitated he was becoming, Noel moved the last two steps up to the young mother, took the paper tri-angle out from under his arm, tore the paper so that the roses were exposed and held out the flowers to the girl. She looked up at exactly that moment, and almost involuntarily, she took the flowers. She took them in both hands.

Now, and moving with a speed and deliberation entirely uncharacteristic, Noel grabbed the stroller with his right hand, the little boy with his left hand and steered around in a circle. Bart had had a MacClaren, so our hero wasn't surprised that the thing maneuvered like an ocean liner. He had managed a very awkward 180, when he remembered that the wheels were locked. He paused, unlocked the wheels and pushed off in the direction of the far side of the terminal, toward Lexington Avenue.

"Where are you going?" the woman asked, alarmed. "What do you think you're doing?"

Noel put his head down, kept walking. Now he was out in the big room, under the painted stars. Back behind his right shoulder, he could hear the young mother calling out, but he couldn't see her anymore, which was just as well. "Shithead!" she yelled. "Stop! Stop!" A yupster carrying a briefcase paused and looked at Noel, considering, but did nothing. It's a cliché that Manhattan's live-and-let-live attitude countenances the most unspeakable crimes. What everybody forgets is that in Manhattan, one is also sometimes left alone in public to do the right thing. Which almost never happens in small towns.

The little girl in the stroller wasn't crying anymore; the boy was sobbing now, although he did continue to walk along. He even held tightly onto Noel's hand. When they reached the other side of the terminal and passed under the arch with its display of gate numbers, a policeman appeared. The woman ran up to him, stopped screaming, and began whispering intently and pointing at Noel and the stroller. Noel thought he heard the words "child molester." He broke into an awkward trot, pushing the stroller, and dragging the little boy. Up ahead, through glass doors that were streaked with dust, he could just make out the gray light of a winter sky. It looked as if it were beginning to snow.

Then, all of a sudden, Noel was on the floor. He remembered the sensation from high school football drills. The team is divided into two lines, one to tackle, the other to be tackled. There you are, running along, "Back straight, knees high, eyes front!" the coach yells. "Hit," the coach yells, his voice projected now away, toward another player, and if the squad is any good, you're horizontal. The cop was an old boy, with a belly that Noel could feel through his clothes. The man had strong arms, though, and after knocking his suspect down, he had had slipped him into a half nelson. Noel could smell the tobacco on his assailant's breath, tobacco and beer. The right side of Noel's face was pushed hard against the floor. His lips touched the marble, which was surprisingly cool. He'd bitten the inside of his mouth. Mixed with the grit from the floor, and the taste of stone, he could also taste blood.

"You going to tell me what this is about?" the policeman asked, through clenched teeth.

Noel didn't say anything. He didn't have the wind to speak.

"You married to her?" the cop asked.

Noel said he wasn't "married to anyone. Never have been."

"I suppose you never met her before?" the cop said, his voice sugared with sarcasm.

"That's right," Noel said. "That's exactly right. Now let go of me!"

By now the woman had reclaimed the stroller and had her son clutched in her arms.

Oddly, having met with such violent resistance convinced Noel that he had been right to act. "There might be real danger," Noel told the cop. "We should get people away from here. Out of the station."

"I'm pressing charges," the woman said. "He was trying to steal my child." She was furious. Noel had never had a woman look at him that indignantly without their having first been lovers.

"I'm pressing charges," the woman said. And then she said it again with more conviction. "I'm pressing charges. I'll testify in court," she said. "I'll find the time. My mother will baby-sit. I'll. . . ." She didn't finish the last sentence. Or if she did finish it, Noel didn't hear her, because it was at that moment that the bomb went off.

First there was a single, ripping boom, a white flash, like summer lightning; the floor shook under Noel's jaw, and there followed the secondary sounds of glass breaking, large objects toppling over. Almost immediately somebody began to call out for water. Then a lot of people were screaming, and the crowd started to run by on its frantic way to Lexington Avenue.

Noel lay there on the floor. He still couldn't quite believe that an actual bomb had gone off. Although obviously there were other people less crippled by a faith in the banality of life. The West River High School Heavenly Choir flew past in a body, white bobby socks flashing, pleated skirts in the air. Noel tried to sit up. "Nope!" said the cop and drove a big fist into the small of his captive's back. This took the wind out of Noel again and he lay down, resigned and almost thankful. Another policeman appeared. One cop talked to the other, nodded at the young mother, and then Noel was on his feet, handcuffed and being frog-marched, double-quick, out toward the Lexington Avenue entrance. They didn't go into the street, though, they veered right, right again, down the incline to the lower level, and through a green wooden door Noel had never noticed before. This opened into a small, square windowless room with fluorescent lighting and a half a dozen Creamsicle-orange plastic chairs set up in two rows. A third cop, much younger than the other two and with brown hair in a brush cut, appeared, and the whole team, working together, cuffed Noel's hands to the metal legs of one of the chairs. A set of handcuffs was used to attach each wrist. Noel realized almost immediately that as long as he sat, he was trapped, but that if he stood and flipped the chair, he would be free. The fat cop and his first accomplice left, and the young one with short hair walked across the room, drew his gun, and stood, facing Noel but looking at the ground. The gun was a revolver. This was before the widespread popularity of the nine-millimeter Gloch.

Noel wanted to know if he was going to be charged with anything, and if so what.

The policeman didn't respond.

Noel began to work the cuff on his right hand down toward the bottom of the chair leg.

The cop pointed his gun at Noel's chest, wagged his head. "Naughty, naughty," he said.

A couple of minutes later the door burst open and two more policemen came in with Che. Noel noticed that the flesh around his writer's left eye was discolored. He too was handcuffed. They fastened him to a chair near, but not the one next to, his editor.

Throughout this procedure, the young cop kept the gun trained at Noel's head. One of the new policemen said, "It's a fucking mess up there. It's 'Nam come home." Then the two cops who had brought Che went back out into the terminal.

The policeman left on guard put his gun back in his holster and lit a cigarette. Noel noticed that there was another door in the room. It was in the wall opposite the one through which they had all come. He supposed it must lead deeper into the bowels of the old building. Through this door, he thought he could hear the faint sound of distant music.

Elevator music, he thought.

Now Che was talking. "I really am honor bound to consider changing publishers," he said.

Noel didn't respond.

"Acropolis is not a first-rate house," he said. Then he turned to Noel. "Outside of diet books, what have you published recently that anybody read?"

Again Noel didn't speak.

"Speak up," said Che. "Cat got your tongue?"

Noel took a deep breath. "Acropolis may not be a first-rate publisher," he said evenly, "but neither are you a first-rate writer. Or a second-rate writer either for that matter."

"I don't have to be," said Che. "I'm the Wordsworth Bomber. I'm the flavor of the month, the hottest thing since Charles Manson."

"Sure, sure," said Noel. "And I'm Idi Amin. Who do you think you're kidding? You couldn't kill a rabbit in a fair fight."

Che smiled seraphically: "I've signed nothing. You and I have spent time together, and we have some few beliefs in common. We both admire the poems of William Wordsworth, for instance."

Now Noel was exasperated. "You think that because they arrested you, everybody's going to assume you set the bomb? And even assuming they're foolish enough to think you set off this bomb, why would they also think you set off all the others?

"Because I set the bomb. They are going to assume I built and detonated the other explosives, because I built and detonated many other explosives."

Noel snickered at this point. He actually snickered. "You don't look anything like the guy. I've seen the police sketch. He's handsome."

"Maybe I don't look like my pictures," said Che. "A lot of celebrities don't look like their pictures. Before today, I'd already killed twenty-nine people. I'm the point man for a national party."

"National party?" Noel said in bewilderment.

"The Know-Nothings won't be called the Do-Nothings anymore," Che said. "Not after today."

"So you're going to be famous," said Noel, "because you killed people who were waiting on line to buy Diet Coke."

Che smiled. "Yup, and because I wrote a book. A book which you didn't think worth publishing."

"Bullshit!" said Noel. "It's not a book yet. Even if you were the famous bomber, you haven't killed that many. *New York Newsday* ran a chart. I think it's twenty-five people."

"They didn't report all the bombings," said Che. "Some of them were passed off as accidents. They weren't accidents. They were bombs. Bombs that I made. And detonated. And I can prove it."

Noel didn't say anything. He just sat back in his Creamsicle-colored chair.

Now Che was talking to himself. Out loud to himself. "There was no TV. I called all the networks, but they didn't come. They didn't believe me."

Noel nodded. "I'm not surprised. You're not exactly a source close to the administration."

"It doesn't matter, though," Che told himself. "They'll certainly put me on TV now. They'll put me on TV for as long as I want."

At this point the young cop tossed his cigarette down on the floor and stamped it out with one black shoe. "Will you two peanuts zip it up?" he said.

Che turned his attention to the guard. "You're Irish, right?"

The policeman didn't say anything.

"Or Italian?"

Still no response.

"Why are you a cop?" Che asked.

The policeman shrugged, lit another Marlboro.

"Because there's so much crime," Che said. "Why's there so much crime? Because we'll let anyone into this country? Why will we let everyone into this country? In order to artificially depress the wages of the working man. Why keep wages down? To make the rich richer."

The cop still didn't say anything, but his eyes were moving, and Noel could tell he was listening, maybe even agreeing. The officer put out the second cigarette, although it was brand new, and he took the gun back out of his holster, began idly to twirl the chamber.

"Let me guess," said Che. "You don't like Jews, do you?"

The policeman shrugged.

"I did it for you!" Che crowed. "Working stiffs like you and me don't have a chance in this world. It's a Jewish conspiracy. Read John Buchan. The rich get richer, the Jews get richer. The niggers keep us down. I'm going to put an end to that. I'm your friend. I'm the workingman's friend," he said. The cop seemed interested.

"You know people have been writing about the international Jewish conspiracy for years," Che said. "Whenever it comes up nowadays, the theory gets ridiculed. But you know why they've been writing about it for years?" he said. "Because it's been around for years. Where there's smoke, there's fire. You know that all three major religions consider usury a sin. And yet this country, this entire country, this Christian country, is leveraged to within an inch of its life."

"But no more," said Che, acting as if the policeman had agreed with him. "Or at least it's going to be acknowledged from now on. We're just about to blow the lid off of it."

Still nothing from the cop.

"Come on," said Che. "Tell me you like kikes. Tell me you like niggers. Just say it. Repeat after me. I like niggers."

Still nothing from the policeman. Nor did he scowl. He did get up out of his chair. He walked over to Che and suddenly, ruthlessly, hit him hard on the top of the head with the barrel of his gun. This made a sound, like a metal rod hitting a pumpkin. Che bleated in pain.

"I like kikes," said the cop. "I like niggers." Then he went back to his chair and sat.

"Christ," said Che. "That hurt, asshole. You're going to be sorry for that."

"Shut the fuck up," said the cop.

"Or what?" said Che.

"Or else you'll try to escape," said the cop. "And I'll be forced to shoot you dead."

So Che shut up. And for a couple of minutes, he actually looked discouraged. Then you could see him figuring out that it didn't really matter what this one cop said. "I'm famous now," he said. "People care what I think. Barbara Walters will be asking me questions about my childhood. I'll be on *Larry King Live*. People don't care what you think, Pig," he said.

The cop stood again; Che subsided.

Shortly after this last outburst, a second policeman appeared. He released the editor from his chair and led him to the door of the inner room. There he stood and knocked. "You want him now?" he asked through the door. "In a minute," said a voice Noel thought he must have heard before. And then, "All right. Bring Mr. Nobody inside."

So the policeman opened the inner door, and Noel was ushered across the second threshold. The room was very much like the first: square, windowless, and illuminated by the plangent orange of a bank of fluorescent lights in the ceiling. There were more Creamsicle-orange chairs. The wall with the door in it was lined with tin filing cabinets, one of which had an antique black fan on it, whose single blade spun busily. There was also a large wooden table, heavily varnished and deeply scarred. This looked as if it had been made to match the benches in the old terminal waiting room. Sitting on the edge of the table, beside a box stereo and talking on a white plastic telephone, was a black man. The man had his back to Noel as the prisoner came in. He was wearing gray flannel slacks and a blue Brooks Brothers shirt. The sleeves of his shirt were rolled up, revealing muscular forearms.

The cops led Noel to one of the plastic chairs, cuffed him, and left.

Then the black man put down the telephone and turned to face his captive. Noel caught his breath.

"Hi, No," said Tom, smiling grimly.

Then there was a knock on the door.

"Come in," said Tom.

The big old cop, the one who'd tackled Noel, came in with two cans of Diet Coke, put them on the table, and left. Tom walked to a chair near the one Noel was in, picked up a leather jacket, and removed a pint bottle of Bacardi from its right, side pocket.

Then he came over to Noel and undid his friend's handcuffs.

"Are you all right?" he asked.

Noel nodded.

"Larry didn't hurt you?"

"Larry?"

"The one who just came in with the drinks."

"No," said Noel. "Not really. He did what he had to do."

Then Tom took a swig of his Diet Coke.

He nodded toward Noel, who took a sip of his. "No," said Tom, "more."

So Noel took another drink.

Then Tom took Noel's can, topped it off with Bacardi, put his thumb over the hole in the can and turned it over, so that the rum was mixed in with the soda. He then repeated the procedure with his own can of soda. "A Cuba Libre Light," he said and smiled.

Noel took a swig of his drink. The Coke was warm, the rum sweet. The combination was vile. But then Noel found that he was terrifically thirsty.

Tom reached into the pocket of his shirt (the Brooks shirt comes with a pocket now, remember?) and removed a half package of Camels. From this he extracted two cigarettes. He put one behind his ear, lit the other. Then he lit the second cigarette off the first, and passed it to Noel. Then he pulled a chair away from the wall and out in front of Noel's and sat down, leaned forward, the brightly colored soda can in one hand, the cigarette in the other.

"Any questions?" he said.

"I thought you weren't a cop," Noel said. "The first time we met, you told me that you were not a cop."

Tom smiled broadly. "Do you remember what you told me? The first time we met?"

Noel didn't remember.

"The first time we met you told me cops lie," said Tom.

"And you denied it."

"I didn't agree with you or disagree with you," Tom said. "But you knew."

"All right," said Noel. "I'm not in trouble am I? I haven't been killing innocents in my dreams, have I?"

"I don't know," said Tom. "Have you been killing innocents in your dreams?" Then he stood up.

"Yes," said Noel, "I have been killing innocents in my dreams."

Tom turned to face his friend and gave him a warm smile. "Listen kid, there are lots of rules. Can't spit on the sidewalk, can't turn right on red. But frankly, we don't give a shit what you do in your dreams."

"Oh," said Noel, and took a pull on his cigarette.

"You know that asshole?" Tom said, pointing toward the door with the hand that held the half-smoked cigarette.

Noel said he did know that asshole. "Or at least I think I do."

"So far he's killed thirty-four people," said Tom. "Killed them. One little girl in particular kinda got to me."

"The chess prodigy?"

"No," said Tom. "Somebody I knew. Not a figment of the public imagination. In any case, he killed a lot of people, most of them innocent. Crippled others."

Noel said, "He told me he killed twenty-nine people."

"Shithead can't count either," Tom said. "Public schools gone all to hell."

Noel said Che hadn't gone to public school.

Tom shrugged.

"Did he really kill people?" Noel asked.

Tom said he had. "You have trouble believing it?"

"Actually, I do," said Noel. "I didn't think he had the sand to commit murder."

"Oh, I believe it," said Tom. "You don't have to be a hero to murder people."

"You been following him?" Noel asked.

"Not for long enough," said Tom.

"You've been following me?" Noel asked.

Tom shrugged. "Giff did arrange to have you in town tonight. We needed some practice moving you around. It turned out to be a lifesaver. Or at least that's what I hope it'll turn out to be," he said, sitting back down, dropping his cigarette butt to the floor, and putting it out with his shoe. He leaned forward, put the Coke can down on the floor, put a hand on each of Noel's knees. "You know what I want?"

"I suppose," Noel said. "And I suppose I'll do it."

Tom picked up his can of Diet Coke. Took a long swig, wiped his chin with the back of his hand.

"You mean it?" he asked.

"I mean it," said Noel.

"Bravo then!" said Tom. "That was easy," he said. "Giff was right about you. I wouldn't have guessed that it would be this simple to convince you to take such a dramatic step." He pulled Noel to his feet and gave him a long and passionate embrace. Noel stood still, with the soda in one hand, the cigarette butt in the other, smiling awkwardly over his friend's shoulder.

Then Tom pushed Noel away, held him at arm's length, grinning almost fiendishly. "Our hero!" he said, and Noel couldn't be certain, but he thought there were tears in the black man's eyes.

35

A CRY FOR CIVILITY

An hour later, Noel was out in the main concourse again, under the painted stars and part of a police press conference. They led him to the top of the grand staircase, the one modeled after the staircase at the Paris Opera. Then they brought him down the stairs for his presentation. It was a little like a coming-out party. The cameras were going the whole time. Later that night and the next morning, when they ran the story on the TV news, the film was played in slow motion as Noel descended the stairs, so that he looked like a great athlete making a key play, or an Olympic runner breaking the ribbon.

The tableaux is as familiar to us today as depictions of the crucifixion must have been during the Renaissance. In the movies, when the scene first became a cliché, the press was represented by character actors in suits and hats. The men shouted, giant flashbulbs went off. No more giant flashbulbs, or felt hats, although nothing much else has changed since the days of the running board and the Linotype machine. There are now more women in the press corps, elbowing each other, shouting rude questions. Or questions at least. In any case there was nothing Noel saw that evening that he hadn't witnessed a hundred, hundred times before. The attention was flattering and frightening in the same instant, and in roughly equal portions. He had the taste of salt in his mouth, but it was blood he was tasting this time, his own sweet blood, not pretzels.

The police made a little self-congratulatory speech, and then deplored the destruction and loss of life Noel had been responsible for. The accused just stood there, bareheaded, looking dazed. Whenever he could catch a cop's eye, Noel would say, "I'm innocent. There has been a terrible mistake," and he'd get back look of almost infinite weariness.

"I have rights," Noel told one of the policemen, finally.

"Not any more, buddy," the cop said. "The man with rights died the day you lit off that first bomb."

Then Tom came up behind him, patted his friend on the shoulder. "Calm down," he said. "You're doing great. You were born for this moment."

Noel was ashamed. "I can't help myself," he said. "I keep saying I'm innocent. All my life, I've been acting guilty, now that I'm charged with something, I keep saying how innocent I am."

"It doesn't matter," Tom said. "Everybody always says they're innocent. You're Sydney Carton, kid. It is a far, far better thing that you do, than you have ever done; it is a far, far better rest that you go to, than you have ever known."

But it wasn't the last line of the book that repeated on Noel then, like a bad meal, but rather higher up the page. "I see a beautiful city and a brilliant people rising from the abyss." That's what he thought, and then he wondered if Carton had had a headache at the end, because he, Noel, certainly had one. Probably from the cigarettes and from the rum.

Before they brought him to the microphone, he played and replayed the interview with Tom. He'd meant to be helpful. He hadn't meant to be this helpful. "You want me to testify against Che?" That's what he'd said after he'd pulled out of Tom's embrace. That's what he assumed they needed.

But Tom had said it was more than that, actually. "We want a little more than that," he'd said and smiled sadly at his friend.

Noel nodded eagerly. He said he could probably provide the court with copies of Che's manuscript, he'd have to check with the lawyers first.

Tom was still nodding, but no longer smiling.

"Noel," he said, finally, "I guess you don't know how serious this is."

Noel stepped back from his friend. "You don't think I did it?" he asked.

Tom reached out, took both of Noel's hands, shook his head.

"So what's the problem?" said Noel.

"You know what that asshole believes?"

"Well I guess he's a Know Nothing."

Tom nodded.

"He has some sort of conspiracy theory. He doesn't like Jews."

Tom nodded again. "You haven't guessed?" he asked.

"Guessed what?" said Noel.

"If we arrest your friend," said Tom, clearing his throat, "and we charge him with the crimes he's committed, he's going to be on TV, telling people what he believes. He's tied up with the Know-Nothings. They'll have a field day. They'll get a couple of million dollars worth of free airtime. And they'll be a banner for every jerk who thinks that other people are the reason for his own, personal unhappiness. Instead of antacid, they'll buy guns."

Noel didn't say anything.

"We're not sure about this, but we think they have charges planted at Indian Point. We know for a fact that they've occupied the place. It looks now like the plan was to have Che announce himself, then threaten to blow the plant. Kill, I don't know, 50,000 people."

Noel nodded.

"We're talking with them. They're waiting for Che to make his announcement, send his manifesto to the press. As soon as he does that, they say they're going to threaten to blow the plant. They want amnesty for Che, of course, and also a meeting, a televised meeting, between their leaders and the president of the United States."

"They won't get it." Noel said.

"They might just," said Tom. "Fifty thousand people. That's a lot of votes."

"Can't you send in a swat team or something?"

"We can, but it would be risky. Better to talk them out of it."

"And how do you plan to do that?"

"It's simple, actually. We just make Che disappear. We stop the message. I think then they'll surrender. Nobody wants to die."

Tom finished off his Diet Coke and took a swig from the Bacardi bottle.

"The Know Nothings have released a statement already," Tom said, after having taking a long drag on his cigarette. "They've announced that they're coming over here this evening in force to talk with press, give the details of each killing, so as to gain credibility. That's what I was on the phone about." He stood, walked around in a circle, and then sat down in his chair, looking sad.

"Why don't you round them all up now?" Noel asked. "Before they talk."

"We can't easily get into Indian Point now," said Tom.

"What about the other ones. The ones who plan to speak with the press?"

"We can't arrest people for their opinions," said Tom. "Not in America." He passed Noel another cigarette and the lighter, a blue plastic butane.

Noel lit the cigarette and took a drag. "So what can you do?"

"I know what I'd like to do," said Tom.

"And what's that?"

"I'd like a doppelganger," Tom said. "A buffer. A cutout. Che goes to jail for some shit we have to think up. Something unglamorous. I don't know. Child molesting."

Then Tom reached over and took Noel by the shoulder. "You take his place. You won't make race an issue. You'll make it something else. I don't give a fuck, actually. Animal rights. Consumer rights. Throw in the environment for all I care, come out against littering, too many commercials on kiddie TV shows."

Noel was nodding right along at this point. "Sounds good at first," he said. "But doesn't that makes me a murderer?"

"You'd get a chance to read the complete works of William Makepeace Thackeray. You might even write that play you've been talking about. We'll give you books. We'll even give you a typewriter."

"You mean I'm going to have to go to jail?" said Noel.

"We picked you for this. Picked you specially," said Tom.

"Jail?" said Noel again.

Tom nodded: "A nice jail. With color TV if you want it. Besides, you're the one told me he liked jail." Now he was smiling broadly. "You'll be famous. A household name. Sidney Carton. Horatius at the bridge."

"It won't be me, though," said Noel. "I won't be myself anymore. I'll be famous for something I didn't do."

"But don't you see?" said Tom, and his smile was triumphant. "That's why we chose you, No. You never were yourself."

Noel Hammersmith stood up suddenly, as if he'd been stung by a hornet. He walked to the other side of the room. "You won't get away with this. The cops all know."

"First place," said Tom, "they don't all know. Second place, and more importantly, what cops know and what cops tell the public: two entirely different things."

"This is a conspiracy you're talking about," Noel said. "A real conspiracy. *Day of the Condor.* Like something out of the movies. You make Watergate look like it was arranged by the Boy Scouts of America. This is a serious attempt to mislead the public."

"Another reason we chose you," said Tom. "The master of diet books." He sat back down and lit himself a new cigarette. This time he didn't offer one to Noel.

Noel reached over to his friend's shirt pocket, removed his own cigarette, held it out and waited for Tom to light the thing. Then he took a long, thoughtful drag. "You've done this before?"

"I'm not authorized to talk about that," said Tom.

"Why not?" said Noel.

"Not important that you know these things."

"That guy we ran with, the weight lifter? The one with the broken nose?" said Noel.

"He filled a slot we had outside of Boston."

"David Berkowitz?"

Tom nodded and smiled. "The creep who escaped from that mental hospital, we talked about it. He was the actual killer."

"I don't exactly follow."

Tom shifted in his chair. "The man who escaped from the mental hospital," said Tom. "He was David Berkowitz. He was the actual genius who shot all the young lovers." Tom pointed at his temple, twirled his finger and rolled his eyes. "The man you saw in all the magazines, the man you saw pictured, and heard interviewed, the man whose adoptive parents you met, he was a cutout. Which is why he looked strangely serene in his pictures. He hadn't murdered anyone. He did what we're asking you to do. That way the real killer got no credit. You commit a serious crime, you lose your right to vote. We think that you should also lose your right to be famous. The real David Berkowitz couldn't bear having some other guy get all the credit. So he escapes and runs right to the nearest newspaper office."

"And?"

"Nobody believed him."

"What about Mark David Chapman?"

Tom shrugged.

"Gary Mark Gilmore?"

"A lot of them were actors before they volunteered," Tom explained. "Failed actors. We favor people like yourself. Solitary individuals, separated from themselves and their surviving families. But with an inchoate desire to do good."

"Christ," Noel said. "You sound like a therapist. How long has this been going on?"

Tom dropped the butt of his new cigarette and stamped it out. "You don't need to know."

"How long exactly has the operation been going on?"

"I can't be specific. It's part of a larger effort. We're doing it to common criminals and to terrorists as well. Wait till we catch Carlos. Remember Carlos, the terrible? When we catch him, he's going to be an old man."

"What about Lee Harvey Oswald?"

"We're not exactly proud of the way that worked out."

"This sucks," said Noel.

"Why's that?" asked Tom. "I felt sure that you of all people would approve."

"But you shot Gary Gilmore in the heart."

"A very special case. The volunteer was seriously ill."

Here I am again in my comfortable 4th floor digs with my IBM Selectric III. Alone in perfect solitude. Willy Loman but this time with his Arthur Miller. With an army of Arthur Millers.

The Know-Nothings were out in force, every other one of them was holding an American flag. They'd set up at the UN. Internationalism is their deadly enemy. Tom was right. The plan was that they would take credit for the killings, name Che as the Wordsworth Bomber, and then announce that their "regular forces" had captured the nuclear facility at Indian Point. Then they'd present their platform.

I didn't cave a moment too soon. They were all set up there in front of the UN and with a healthy press corps in attendance, when the New York City Police announced that Che had nothing to do with the bombings, that Indian Point was still held by Consolidated Edison (this was a bluff), and that the actual Wordsworth Bomber was in their hands and would talk with the press in Grand Central.

The Know-Nothings made a great fuss, but nobody much hung around to listen. Everybody rushed to Grand Central to interview the actual, the real Wordsworth Bomber. Me.

Suspects are not customarily permitted to speak with the press, but the police made an exception this time, in order to belie the pronouncements of the Know-Nothings. They'd been parading me around in handcuffs, but now they cleaned Yours Truly up and presented him with a microphone.

I took questions.

"Was I an active member of the Know-Nothings?"

"The who's?"

"The Know-Nothings."

I'd never heard of them, I lied.

Was I sure? I must have heard of the Know-Nothings.

"Wait a minute," I said. "You mean the people who want to seal our borders, and kill off everybody whose great-grandfather was not born in Oklahoma?"

This got a titter from the press.

"I guess I've heard of them," I said. "I thought that ultimately they were silly people. Not capable of acting, really. Weren't they also called the Do-Nothings?"

"You think that violent action is important?"

"That's right. Without courage no other virtue is possible, except by accident. I had courage. I acted."

By this time a few of the Know-Nothings had arrived in Grand Central and were in the audience hissing me. "He's an impostor," they said. "He's a volunteer. A cat's paw for the international Jewish banking conspiracy. In real life he's a diet book editor."

So one of the reporters asked me that. "Are you a diet book editor? Are you a volunteer, in collusion with the New York City Police Department?"

I said I was a diet book editor. "That's right," I said.

"Are you in collusion with the police?"

And here I kinda slipped up, although it came out all right. "God, but I hope so," I said.

This got a chuckle. Then Tom took the microphone. "We are charging this man with a number of serious crimes. He faces life imprisonment." Then he stepped away. I stepped to the microphone, held up my handcuffs. "Do I look like a volunteer?"

At this point one of the newspaper women got snippy with me. "You have been accused of a multitude of serious crimes. That's the only reason we're speaking with you. I wonder who you think you are, then, to belittle the program of a legitimate political group?"

Looking back now, I think I did pretty well on my feet. I said, "I'm the one who set the bombs these people are taking credit for. I'm also the reason that you all are here, and not across town interviewing Santa Claus."

What was odd about this is that I was really beginning to think I had committed the crimes. Play a part and you become it. And so at first I was exhilarated. Then I was filled with remorse.

At first I couldn't figure out what to say. Then I remembered the weight lifter. I told them about the loss of the Brooks Brothers Blue. I told them how I hated the language of the IRS. I mentioned the fattening diet pills, the shatterproof clocks that I had shattered, the leaky ballpoint pens. "We find ourselves living in a house of cards," I said. "I'm for the dignity of man," I said. "I don't want to be a clerk, or a machine. I don't want to be beautiful like the people in commercials. I want to be a man among men. A person among other people, a face in this magnificent crowd."

And then some reporter, bless her imagination, she stood up and I pointed to her. "So all these killings," she said, "they were really a cry for civility?" I think she meant an irony, but it didn't come out that way. I just nodded. And there it was the next day, in more than half my headlines: "A cry for civility."

36

PRIZE PIG

IT'S BEEN LESS than forty-eight hours and some hotshot reporter has discovered about my parents having been killed by a bomber in Israel years ago. Now suddenly, my character is clear as glass. The explanations are all so pat. Sure, my parents died. That was bad. I hated it. That's not why I killed thirty-four people. Or it wouldn't be why I killed thirty-four people, if I had killed thirty-four people, which I did not do.

I had worried at first that the press would uncover the little ruse Tom Janus and I are engaged in, but the more time passes, the more assured I become. A story, like a large stone rolling downhill, gains in momentum as it grows in size. A day ago, it might have been possible to convince somebody of my innocence. That time has passed. Everybody who's anybody has written the story at least once now. They're all invested in it. The saga of my life is big business, my wickedness a brand name product.

I recall a documentary in which the young Marlon Brando spoke of the news business. He said, "People don't realize that a press item, a news item is money, and that news is hawked in the same way that shoes are or toothpaste or lipstick or hair tonic or anything else."

I saw the documentary at an art house and thought Brando was a wise man, if a little cracked. Today he seems starkly sane, a voice in a wilderness of noise.

What's fascinating to me, to a person who has always had difficulty with faith, is how much faith the purportedly atheistic members of the media seem to have in the GREAT CHAIN OF CIRCUMSTANCES. They don't call it God, they call it science, and pride themselves on having no system, on random sampling. But there's nothing random or scientific about their sampling. They have made a deity of passivity. People act only because they are acted upon. I no longer expect them to actually figure out that I am a fraud. The cards are carefully stacked against that. But I had expected that somebody would stumble on the concept of free will. Not one columnist, not one pundit has even considered the possibility.

"Looking into the past of this unfortunate young man one can't help but make out the shapes of his future violent acts," one of them wrote. What a lot of nonsense. My parents had nothing to do with who I am today.

They got Cleo's notes, incidentally, and ran that quote I gave her about wanting to be a sort of modern Buddha, to sit quietly and read my clips. They bribed one of the guards, sent him in with a camera, and ran a picture of me sitting on my metal bunk, reading my clips. "Media Buddha" was the caption. "Sociopath's dream comes true."

At first the articles were relatively accurate, if sketchy. Then the facts were amplified for dramatic purposes and, finally, in an attempt to keep the story alive, they were altered beyond recognition. Read the current copy and you'd think I was brought up by Mister & Mrs. Frankenstein. "Even as a small boy, Noel Hammersmith had a bomb nestled against his heart," one of them wrote, going on to "document" a series of violent incidents that were supposed to have taken place in "the rectory from hell." They got that phrase from Tony, who seems to have an avocation at last in talking to the press about "his dear friend," a man whose letters he couldn't find the time to answer. But now he's dug them up, and sold them, with comments, for a good deal of hard cash.

The painful childhood is his particular angle. This doesn't just explain me, but also my sister. How could somebody not cracked in the head desert the fabulous Fulton Basque Holloway?

And once he started the ball rolling, everybody's come forward to say what a miserably unhappy child I was. Which I don't remember having been. We had that incident with the dead squirrel. My father hit me then, but it was only because I had almost killed us both. The only other time my father ever hit me was with a football. He'd throw it in my general direction, I'd fail to catch it, and the ball would bounce off my chest.

They were decent parents, both of them. I wish they hadn't died. Especially, I wish they'd never had a second child. But few cultures, outside of contemporary China, have ever considered having a second child to be a punishable offense.

It's true that my father believed in God, but even this, while perhaps considered gauche in polite society, is not wicked. Piety can be a bore, but I'm not sure piety alone can ever constitute abuse.

The word *genius* is often linked with my name in the popular press. The columnists all report that I'm clever, devilishly clever, and that I have suffered, suffered greatly. Clever? Because I built bombs? What if I'd built paper airplanes instead? Or models of wooden sailing ships? Would that be clever? I'm clever simply because I've gotten their attention. Which says more about how highly the Fourth Estate values itself than about my particular IQ. As for the suffering, in the past I always felt that I had suffered; now that other people are saying it, I can't remember exactly when or even how.

––––––––––––

Same typewriter. Same cell. Same writer. But a week has passed. I'm in a federal prison in lower Manhattan. It's a new, clean facility, built in 1977. I'm in federal because I've been charged with having transported explosives across state lines in order to kill people. I'm in solitary because I'm high profile. It's felt that I might be hurt by other prisoners, which—because I'm so well known—would be an embarrassment. I am, after all, the prize pig.

37

MANY, MANY
BEAUTIFUL WOMEN

Sitting at my new metal desk. A desk uncluttered with manuscripts. I've always wanted a metal desk. And built right
in. But everything is built in here. Built to last. The uniform is horrid. It's a jumpsuit with snaps. Made of canvas and
dyed the color of a baboon's ass. Tom arranged for me to have
soft jockey shorts, so at least the thing doesn't chafe. I got two
dozen pairs of shorts. That's twelve to wear and twelve to barter.
They're almost as valuable as cigarettes. It was arranged to have
my jumpsuits washed repeatedly. This also helps enormously.

I have one real concern, which is that the other prisoners will
gang up and murder me. They're big, mean, and intensely masculine. Probably they sense that I am other.

I spend most of my time alone in my room. Just as a writer
must do. It's a small room, a single, with bed, sink, and toilet.
And everything is rock solid. This toilet is securely fastened. No
mortgage, low maintenance. Living accommodations that Henry
David Thoreau might have approved of. Simplify, simplify.

I don't see the other prisoners much but have a kind of awe
for them. They frighten me, but it's not simple fear. There's a lot
of noise about freedom in the outside world, but nobody much
does anything about it. Most of us give it up to the first girl, or
corporation, that comes along and will have us. Not here. Many

of my new colleagues are nutso, but the ones who aren't nutso
are quite dramatically brave.

The exercise yard is on the roof. It's walled in, and the walls
are topped with wire. A couple of months ago, two fellow matric-
ulants hid out up there. When the guards left, they climbed
through the wire and jumped. The building is eleven stories
high. They both died. Apparently this happens often. Only one
jumper has ever survived, and that was because he landed on the
dead body of the man who leaped right before he did. The sur-
vivor had to be transferred to Danbury. We're not equipped to
handle wheelchairs.

My classmates scare me, but they also inspire me. There's a
palpable splendor to a man who's done what he needed to do,
and then been caught. Don't get me wrong. They're probably
horrid people. But who knows? All we know for certain is that
they're antisocial. Is it necessarily bad to reject the society we
now live in?

In the meantime, this same world, which has locked men up
for embezzlement and for crimes of passion, has made of me a
hero. That's right. I'm famous. I'm not Lee Harvey Oswald or
Elizabeth Taylor yet, but I'm already neck and neck with Gary
Mark Gilmore. I get suck-up letters from Norman Mailer.
Remember *The New York Post* with that picture: Sam Sleeps?
Well, I've been in the *Post* twice. Even *New York Newsday* put me
on the cover. They had me stretched out in my cot, reading a
Penguin edition of *Henry Esmond,* with the headline "No Man's
Land." Not an unbecoming picture either.

––––––––––––––––––

I don't know if it's all the press, the not running, or what, but my
spirits are beginning to lift. Not just lift, but soar. My body's getting a rest, the first real rest in years. My legs ached for a couple
of days. Then they tingled. Now they feel great. Not running is

every bit as addictive as running ever was. Also, it seems to be
better for you. Or at least it's better for you if have a bad ankle.

I have *The New York Times* daily delivery. The people on 43rd
Street gave me a free subscription. I guess they're considering
using me in an advertisement. In any case it's free, and it's here.
When I'm tired of reading about my own case, I can study up on
other important developments. The news doesn't gall me the
way it did. I now assume that most of the stories about others are
just as far off the mark as are the stories I've been reading about
myself. I had always suspected that the press refracted its sub-
jects, but I had no idea. It's a far, far better world than the one
you read about in the daily disappointment.

I don't mean to be a Pollyanna, but there's no denying the
distortion. The world is nothing like the one you see every day in
the newspapers and on television. Just take me, for instance,
Yours Truly. They've made me a hero. Not for my good qualities,
and I have some, but for my worst ones.

The forgiveness of sins indeed. The resurrection of the body.
The life everlasting. All this in a steel cell that goes ten feet one
way and twelve another.

Of course it's not all praise. Some members of the serious
press have taken potshots, called me "cold blooded and mania-
cal." But when you consider my actual character, this is not
unflattering.

From Ginny they found out about Pedro, that little boy I
used to send money to. Some anonymous philanthropist has set
up a trust fund for him. Pedro will come to the States, go to college. Harvard and Yale are competing for him. When this was
announced, there was a good deal of tisking at me from editorial
pages about how I had abandoned true charity in favor of despicable "limelight-seeking violence." On the other hand, it was the
limelight-seeking violence that got Pedro his scholarship.

The TV news shows run and rerun the eight-millimeter films
my long-dead bachelor uncle took of my fifth and sixth birth-
days. You see the stripling hero getting his first two-wheeler, a

Raleigh. I loved that bicycle. My mother let me keep it in
the bedroom for a week. It was an English racer, forest green, and
my feet didn't reach the pedals. These films were taken before
I got fat, before my sister was born. I'm laughing, hugging
and kissing my parents. "For he's a jolly good fellow, for he's
a jolly good fellow, for he's a jolly good fellow, which nobody
can deny."

I'm supposed to be a murderer, but the feeling I get from my
public is not one of hatred, or scorn. It's one of interest, and
sometimes even respect. It's not exactly as if I were being
accused of saving all those people who died, instead of killing
them, but it's close enough to make no nevermind. Everybody's
interested, and most everybody's sympathetic.

Time has passed. I've been writing, but not in my journal. I'm
trying to keep up with my mail. I get a couple of hundred pieces
every week. The truly passionate love letters are from women
who have never met me. Quite a few fans have sent photographs
of themselves in bathing suits. I don't know, because packages
aren't allowed, but according to the guards, several of the women
have sent me their underwear. And it's not just the kooks who
like me. Many of my keenest admirers have jobs and husbands.
Good jobs, good-looking husbands. Could this many beautiful
women all be wrong? What's really gratifying is that all of my old
girlfriends have now fallen hard for the man they once thought
an insufferable prig. Polly sent a long, handwritten letter. "Dear
Boy Saint," it began. Ginny has offered to start up where we left
off. "I know we didn't get along on the outside, but now that
you're in jail, we might have the perfect relationship," she wrote
in an uncharacteristic burst of candor.

Wilson sent a card from Bart. She wrote the card, and for all I
know, she also made up the message. Still, I was moved: "Dear
Da, Da, we miss you. Marry us. "

Ginny is going to have a show at a gallery downtown, not far from here, actually. She painted me from old snapshots, for the cover of *Newsweek* and has written a brief description to go along with it about my "deep dish masculinity."

Even my Judas, Fay of the very Green Eyes is passing herself off as heartbroken. "He was my dearest friend, and mentor," she told the reporter for *The New York Times Magazine* section. "A brilliant manager. A younger, better looking version of Maxwell Perkins. A genius without cigarettes or hats." Of course I smoke now. Everybody in prison smokes.

———

This is my fifth day without coffee. Giving it up would have been harder, except that the coffee here is so bad. I had headaches, terrible headaches. Tom smuggled in some Sinutab. I'm over the hump, and now am very proud of myself. And close to serene. I'm afraid the stimulants were part of the problem. I was always up, and always about to crash. Being calm makes faith more likely. I remember those long-ago Saturdays, when my father used to take me fishing. "Being a clergyman is a lot like fishing with worms." That's what my father used to say.

"Faith and hope are often confused," he used to say. "Like love and hate, they exist on opposite sides of the coin. Hope is always all about the person doing the hoping. Hope sells self-help books. I hope I get over breast cancer. Now. I hope I get rich. Now. Hope buys lottery tickets," he said. "Hope works eighty-five hours a week at a white shoe law firm. Faith gardens, faith goes fishing, faith plays with the children."

Giff has visited twice. He's seeing Kat. I guess they've been a regular item for a month or so now. And my old friend, my dear old friend, is beginning to have bags under his eyes. I like Giff, but he seems less splendid to me now than he did on the outside. I still admire the style, but also I can see how taxing it is to keep up that image. Adultery isn't just very wicked, it's also very very hard work.

And speaking of work, a literary agent appeared yesterday. He got right into the cell with me. I have no idea how. Probably cost him twenty cartons of cigarettes. He looks like an English mobster, hair slicked back, but a good suit, all natural fabrics. He represents most everybody literary. Saul Bellow, William Maxwell, Philip Roth. Everybody but God. He smokes a kind of cigarette with silk in the title. Something silks. Silk Cuts. Outside of the carton of cigarettes, he brought me two coffees and a bagel with cream cheese. He reported that Zaro's has named a muffin after me. "The No Muffin" it's called, and it's supposed to be spectacularly low in fat. I gave the guard my coffee, and bagel.

AGENT: "I should have brought you one of those muffins."

"It's all right," I said. "I'm not a star fucker."

The agent wanted to know what I had written.

I told him that I had meant to write for the stage, but I hadn't actually finished any plays. "First I thought every play should be three acts. So I wrote two acts and couldn't start the third. Then I talked with a friend who told me that a one act play was perfectly respectable. Then I found that I couldn't finish one act either."

AGENT: "So these plays you're talking about, these unfinished plays, they lack a final form?"

"That's right."

AGENT: "They're random. In the same way that life is random."

"I suppose."

AGENT: "How much material altogether?"

"I've probably got 300 pages."

AGENT (lighting another cigarette for himself): "How many plays?"

"Wait a minute. Let me think. There must be eighteen," I said, and lit one of my own cigarettes.

AGENT: "Some better than others?"

"Maybe."

AGENT: "Lose five."

"Five?"

AGENT: "That's right. We'll call the book *A Baker's Dozen*.

"And do you have a particular publisher in mind?"

AGENT: "Knopf ring any bells."

Of course I went for it. They are going to publish the plays. Turns out that contract was part of a ploy to get at my journals, which are what they really want. What they're dying for. The essence of me. That's what they want. Can you imagine?

All because of an asshole named Che Guevara. An asshole who is now moldering away on Rikers Island, awaiting trial on charges of molesting a fictional innocent, and boring the guards and his fellow prisoners with protestations about his importance. Tom went and saw him and came to me with a very funny picture. "He keeps saying, 'I'm the malefactor. I'm the Wordsworth Bomber,' which everybody at Rikers thinks is a scream."

I forget now if the Son of Sam bill has been overturned, or if my clever new agent simply found a way around it, but I am going to have a say in what happens to the money from all these publications. Whatever editor they hire, he or she has to be paid, but there will still be a good deal in the pot. Much more than I could have made if I'd worked a dozen dull lifetimes at Acropolis. I can set up a scholarship fund for Bart, send him to the school of his choice. The leftovers will go to Planned Parenthood.

I'm thinking I'll write a real play now. All three acts. Turns out I love to write. Especially now that I have an audience. My words have become precious. For once in my life I have the sympathy, nay the adoration, of women. Many, many beautiful women.

38

I WAS RIGHT

TOM SHOWED UP last night to say that NBC was running a two-hour special titled "Real Monsters," and that I was going to be the featured monster. Giff was supposed to come as well but canceled at the last minute. He's been making himself very scarce. I told Tom the TV on this floor is busted, and he said that was okay, because I could go down to 3 and watch in the common room.

I told him I didn't know about "mingling, around here. I do kind of stick out."

TOM: "I'll be with you."

There must have been twenty to thirty prisoners sitting in white plastic chairs, watching a TV that was on a high stand, like in a hospital. But in this case the thing was chained to its shelf.

We came in with a guard, right as the show began, and stood back around ten feet behind the crowd. Then a giant black guy with tear tattoos on his cheek saw me. He nudged a little ferrety white guy sitting next to him. The ferrety one reached to the row in front of him and touched another man who also turned and looked our way.

The COs don't carry guns anymore. When they did carry guns, the prisoners would sometimes knock them down, take their guns, and shoot them dead. So the one guard with us was unarmed. Tom is fit, but he's no giant. The guard had a walkie-talkie, of course, and you can call for help with a walkie-talkie. We were locked in, though, locked away from any backup the guard might have called.

The prisoners began to stand. First Tattoo, then ferret, then the rest. They all turned to face us, gave their backs to the TV. I didn't say anything. Tom didn't say anything either, but I could hear him breathing. The guard was fiddling furiously with his walkie-talkie. Then the big black guy began to clap. The others joined in, first slowly, and then faster. Finally they were cheering as well. Some prisoners picked up the chairs and banged them on the floor. The big guy with the tattoo moved out of the crowd, came to my side, and raised one of my arms in the air. All the other prisoners roared. Sounded like the background of my Johnny Cash album.

At that moment three more guards burst onto the floor. When they saw what was happening, they stood back against the wall to watch. Looked a little shamefaced.

After everybody was done clapping and hurrahing, the big guy with the tattoos—his name is Allan—gave me his chair. The ferret gave Tom his. Tattoo offered me a cigarette, which I accepted. Ferret lit it. And we all watched the rest of show, which wasn't bad. The guy who was supposed to be me has a cleft in his chin. He's got to be a foot taller than I am. Apparently they plan to make a two-hour TV special. Don Johnson is interested in playing Noel Hammersmith. He's already read the complete poems of William Wordsworth. Or that's what he told the reporter for *People* magazine. He wants to come in and speak with me someday, so as to understand my motivations. I'll tell him "I suffer, I suffer greatly." This is the first time in my life I've ever been willing to say something so morose in public. And just about the first time in my life that it hasn't been true.

Tom came in to tell that "We've got the reintroduction of the Brooks Brothers Blue. They're making suits that fat men can wear." Ten different senators have signed a bill to get the seven-year-old comprehensibility clause written into IRS regulations next year. Pedro has been accepted at Harvard on a full scholarship. Or did I already tell you that? Grand Central Station, once in danger of being torn down, is being restored to its original splendor. They're going to clean the ceiling, take out the stores. The Swiss army knife has a new sort of scissors in the works. The metal flange has been replaced with a device less likely to break. Plus people all over the country are paying each other's tolls.

I'm still in solitary, but now when I pass the other prisoners in the hall, I smile and wave. Mostly they wave back.

I've gone through all of Thackeray's novels. I've also reread Orwell's *Down and Out in Paris and London*. Of course my fondness for *The Tale of Two Cities* has in no way diminished.

Complaints? Well, you can't control the press. Sometimes they do hurt my tender feelings. But then they are also hard on Mother Teresa.

Never have I been so loved. I still get a half a dozen marriage proposals a month. Could this many beautiful women all be wrong? I'm not as assiduous a correspondent as was John Wayne Gacey (unfortunately he was the real thing), but I'm damn assiduous. Write forty letters a week. Try and let them down gently.

Objections? Well, there's the cuisine. Plus you only have a very few minutes to eat. Plus there's something about having a toilet in the room that stays the appetite. So when I went out for my monthly medical checkup this morning, I was expecting good news. Still, I was surprised to find that I'm all the way down to 138 pounds. And this on a doctor's scale. I swore that if ever I got down to 138 pounds I'd be a happy man. And you know what? I was right.

The End